DRAGON BALL

Training with the Master

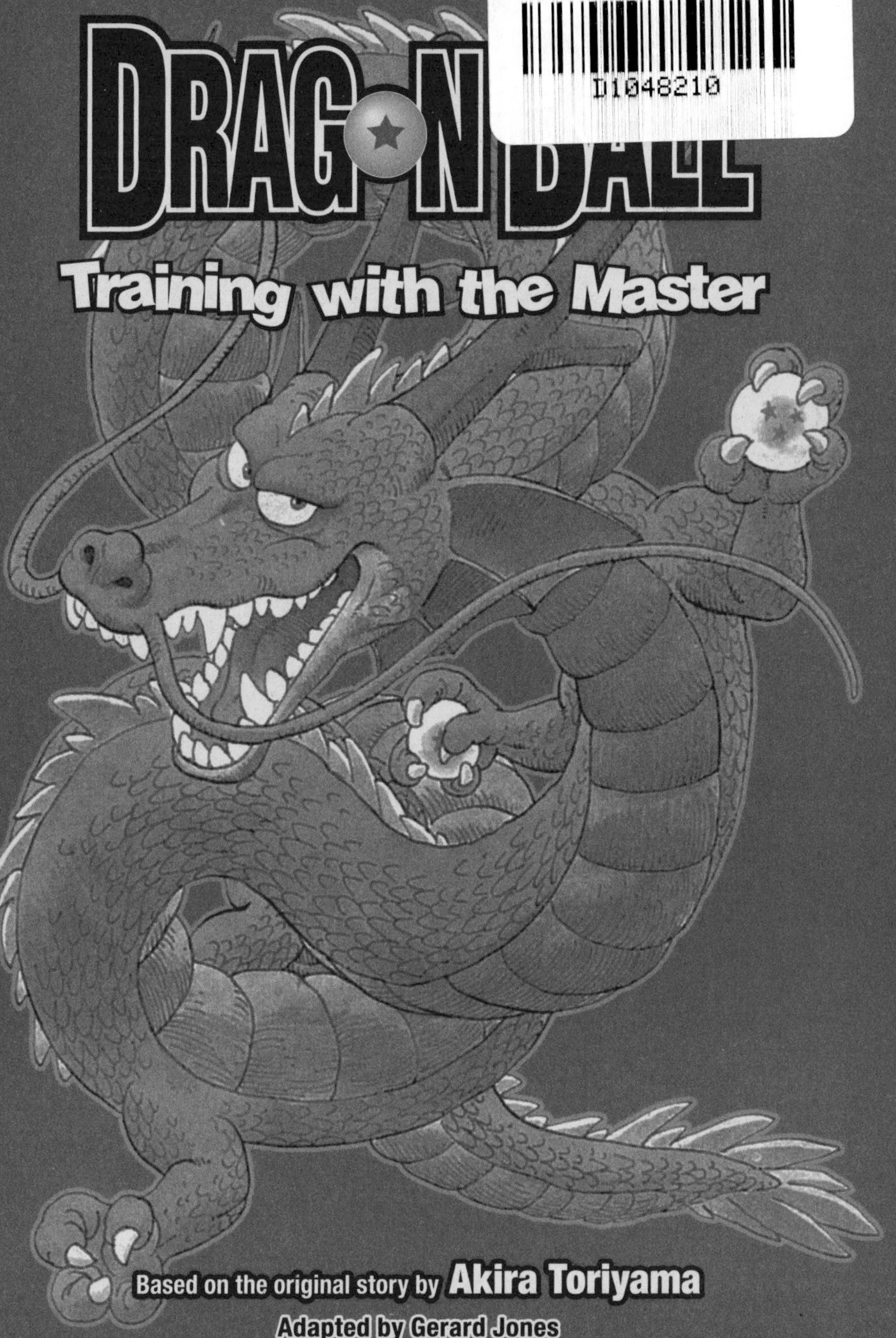

Based on the original story by **Akira Toriyama**

Adapted by Gerard Jones

DRAGON BALL TRAINING WITH THE MASTER
CHAPTER BOOK 6

Illustrations: Akira Toriyama
Design: Frances O. Liddell
Coloring: ASTROIMPACT, Inc.
Touch-Up: Frances O. Liddell & Walden Wong
Original Story: Akira Toriyama
Adaptation: Gerard Jones

Sources for page 78, "A Note About Krillin":

Cable, Amanda, "From Middlesex School Boy to Shaolin Monk: Enter the (Terribly Suburban) Dragon," *Daily Mail Online*
http://www.dailymail.co.uk/femail/article-1085707/From-Middlesex-school-boy-Shaolin-monk-Enter-terribly-suburban-dragon.html
(accessed August 27, 2009)

Shaolin Gung Fu Institute, "What Is Kung Fu?," *Shaolin Gung Fu Institute*
http://www.shaolin.com/StyleContent.aspx?Style=Styles
(accessed August 27, 2009)

Wikipedia contributors, "Shaolin Kung Fu," *Wikipedia, The Free Encyclopedia*
http://en.wikipedia.org/wiki/Shaolin_Kung_Fu
(Accessed August 29, 2009)

Published by
VIZ Media, LLC
P.O. Box 77010
San Francisco, CA 94107

10 9 8 7 6 5 4 3 2 1
First printing, January 2010

www.vizkids.com   www.viz.com

Contents

Who's Who

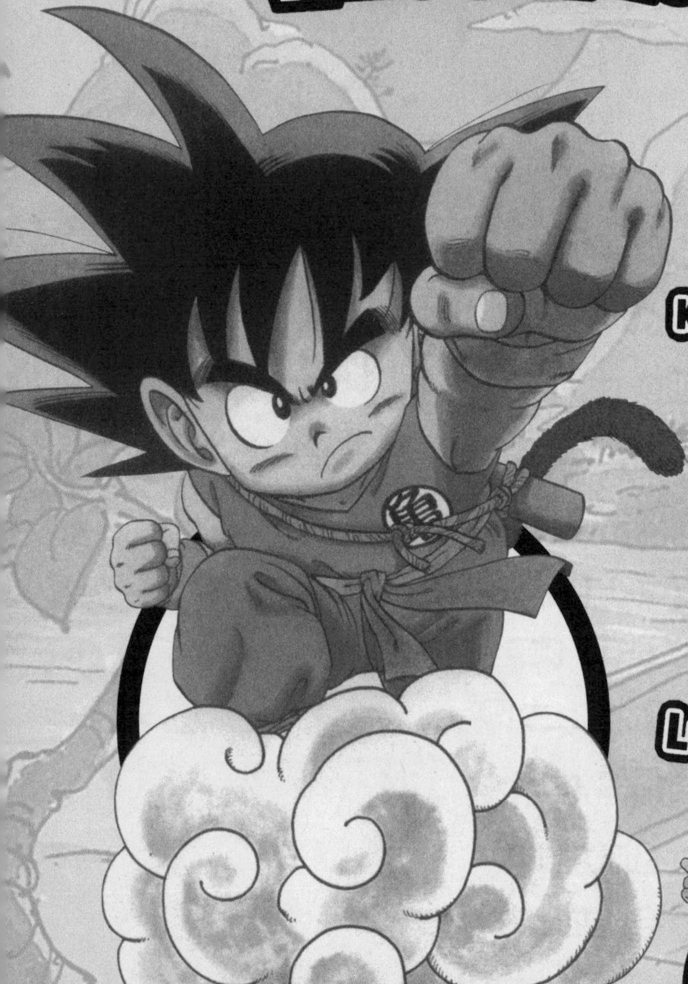

Goku

This kid's come a long way since his days of forest living. He's become quite a warrior with the strength of a big, hairy, apelike beast...and a heart of gold.

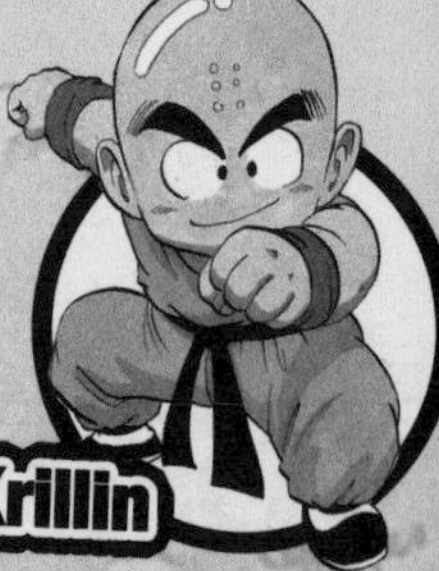

Krillin

Krillin wants Master Roshi to turn him into a martial arts master. He's got skills, but the little baldie's no match for Goku!

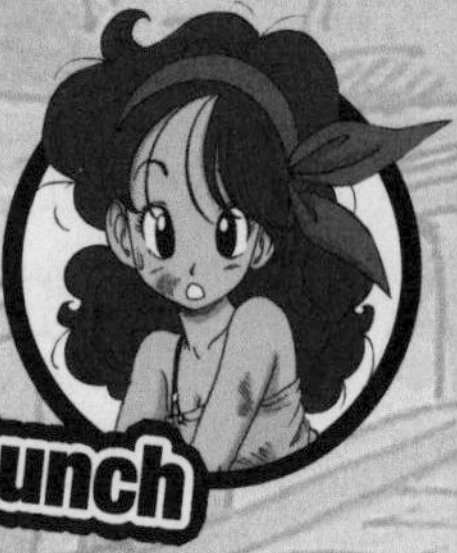

Lunch

Roshi's a lonely guy, and Lunch is good company...but she's got a *nose* for trouble!

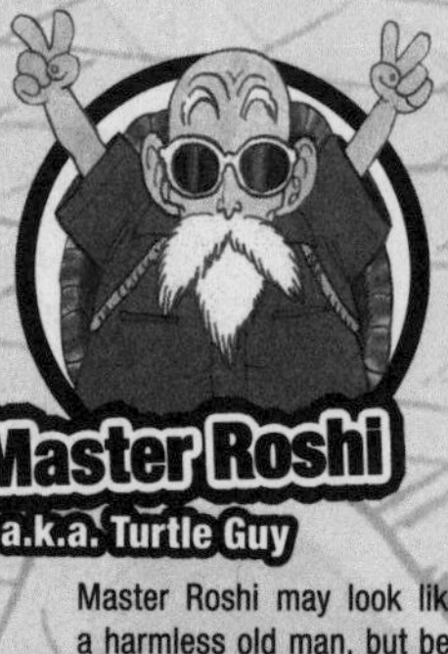

Master Roshi
a.k.a. Turtle Guy

Master Roshi may look like a harmless old man, but behind that mustache he packs a serious Kame-Hame-Ha!

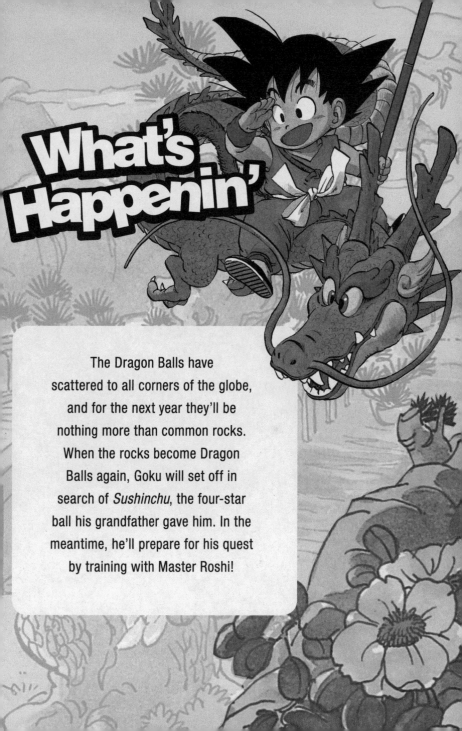

What's Happenin'

The Dragon Balls have scattered to all corners of the globe, and for the next year they'll be nothing more than common rocks. When the rocks become Dragon Balls again, Goku will set off in search of *Sushinchu*, the four-star ball his grandfather gave him. In the meantime, he'll prepare for his quest by training with Master Roshi!

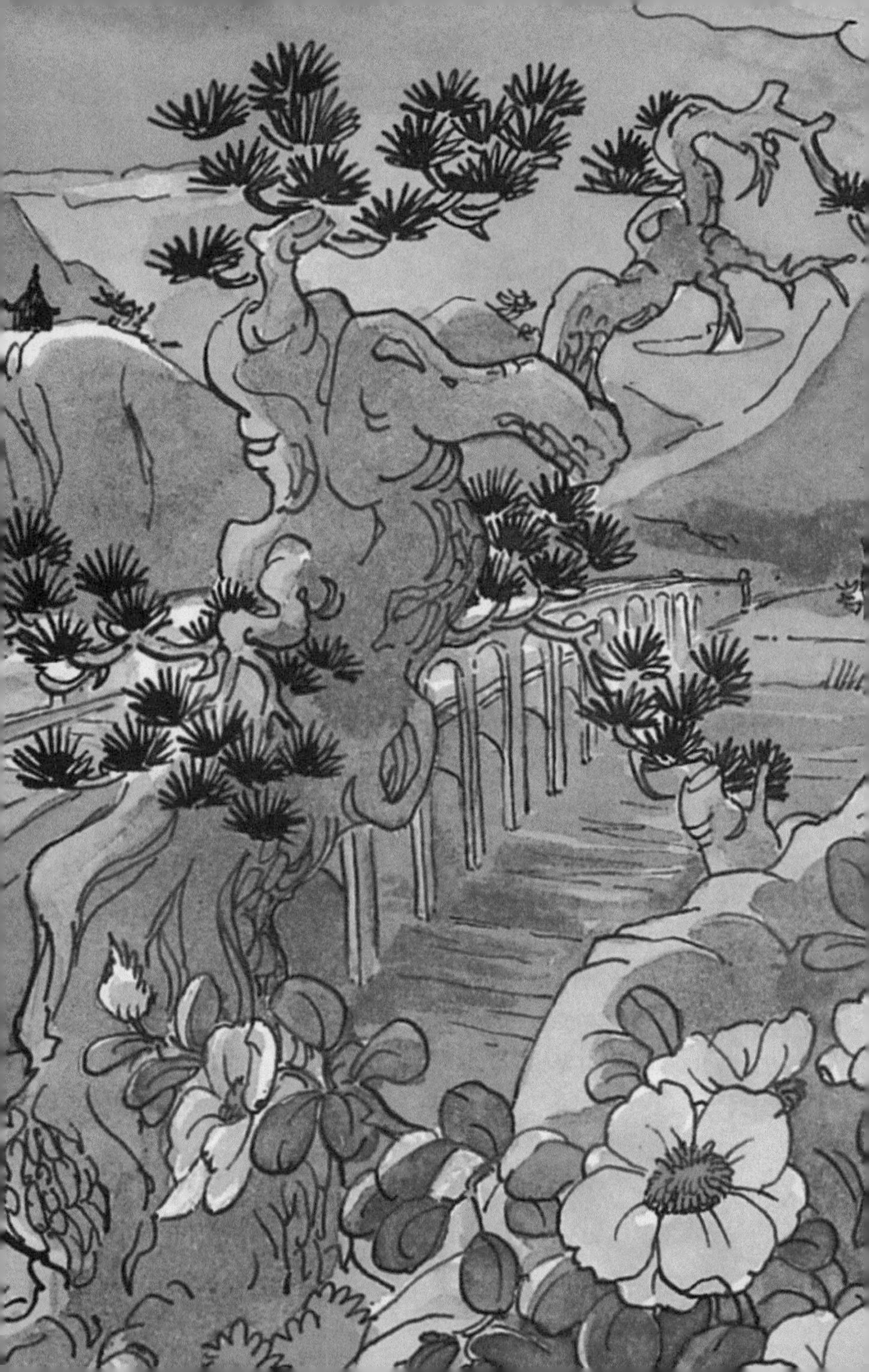

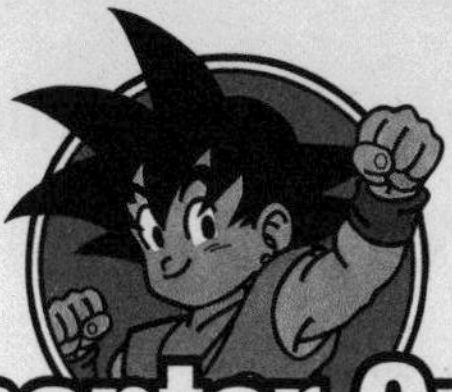

Chapter One

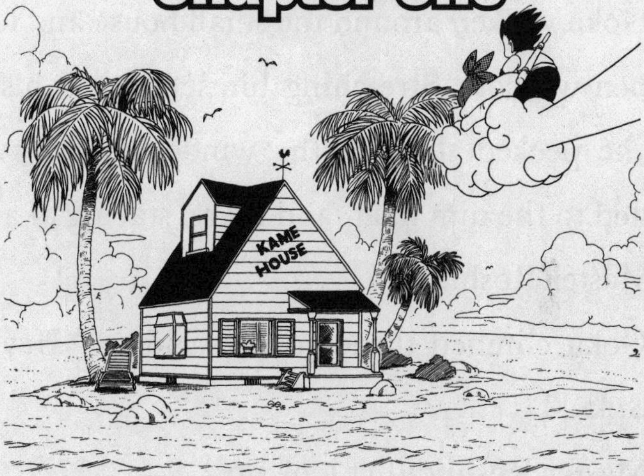
KAME HOUSE

"Aw-right!" Goku cried. "There it is!"

Even though he was riding Kinto'un, it had been a long trip from Goku's little house in the woods to Master Roshi's island. Now Goku swooped low and jumped off the cloud, landing in the sand with a quiet thump. He grabbed the few things he'd packed and balanced them on his head. Kinto'un zipped back into the sky, where it would hover until its master called for it again.

"Hey, old timer!" Goku yelled as he walked to the front door. "It's me-eeeee!"

No one answered.

Goku walked around the small house and found an open window. Stretching himself up on his tip-toes, he peeked through the window. Goku's eyes adjusted to the dim light, and there, staring at a TV, was Master Roshi.

Goku climbed through the window. "Hey! It's me, Goku!"

Master Roshi didn't look up.

Goku came up close to Master Roshi and yelled, "HEY, TURTLE GUY!!!"

"Ork!" cried the old man, jumping straight up in the air. "Don't scare me like that! What are you doing here, anyway?"

"I came to get trained!" Goku grinned.

"Sure, sure, whatever," the old master muttered, turning back to the TV. "Just give me a minute, okay?"

"But I'm hungry!"

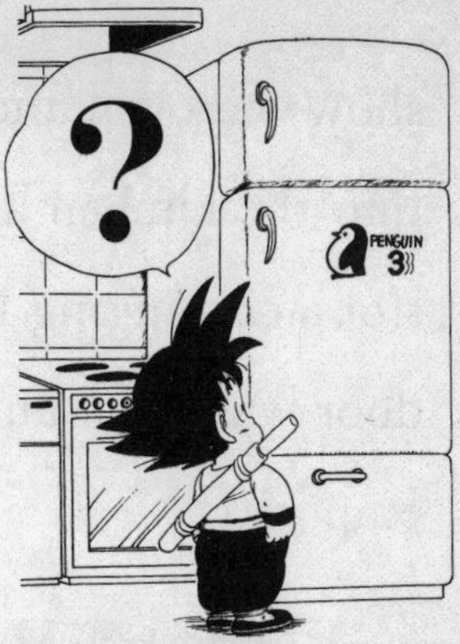
?
PENGUIN 3

"The fridge is right over there." Master Roshi pointed. "Help yourself."

Goku went to the kitchen and opened every cabinet and drawer. Finally, he came to a big white box with a penguin on it. He opened the door and a blast of cold air rolled over him.

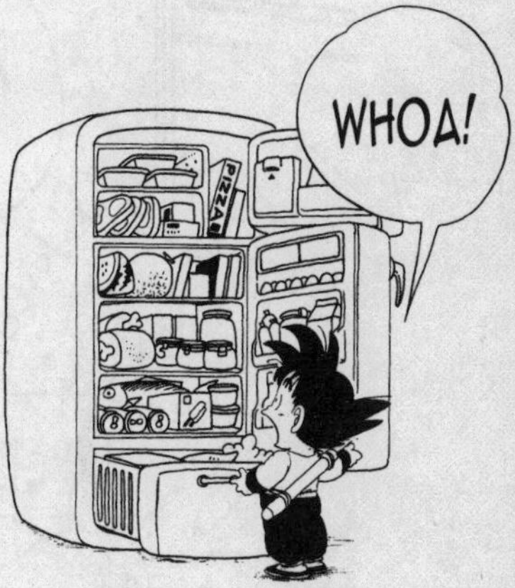
WHOA!
PIZZA

"Whoa!" he cried. "It's like winter in there! But there's plenty of food!"

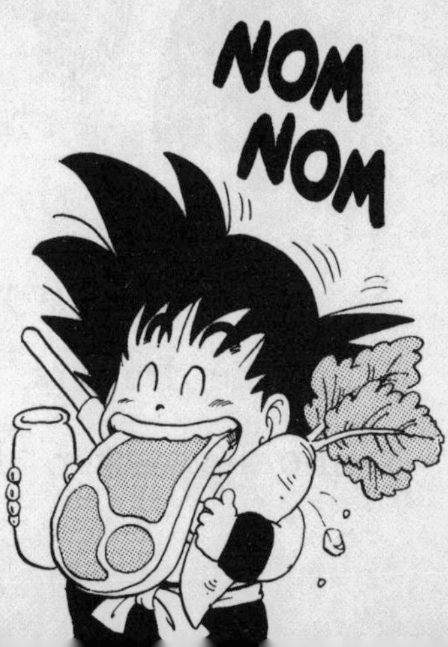
NOM NOM

Goku shoved everything and anything into his mouth. Eggs and meat and carrots and fish. He ate for the whole next hour.

Finally, Master Roshi's

show was over, and it was time for a snack. He walked into the kitchen and found Goku lying on the floor, stomach bulging like a soccer ball. The refrigerator door was open and all the shelves and drawers were empty.

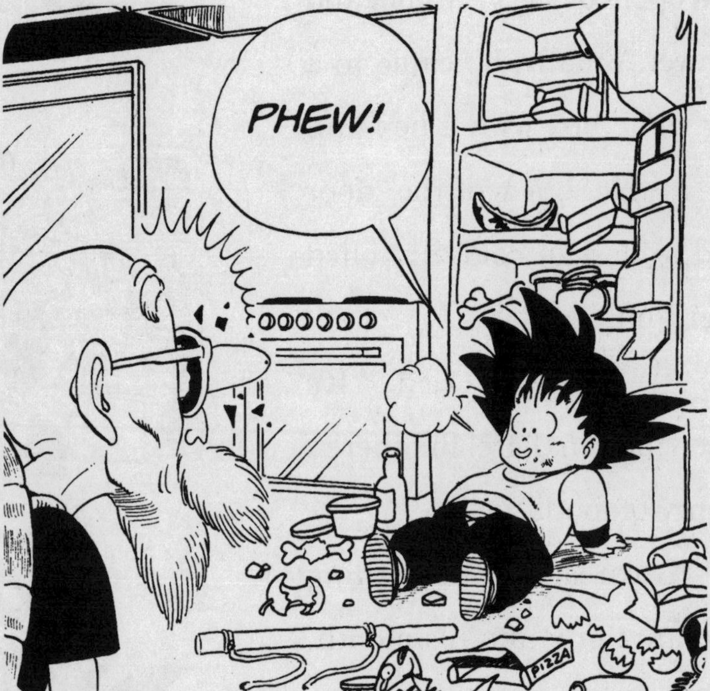
PHEW!
PIZZA

"You ate *everything*?" Roshi squawked. He pulled out the drawers, searched the shelves, and peered into the freezer. "Even the butter?"

"Uh-huh," Goku groaned.

"A whole week's worth of food." Roshi sighed, shaking his head. "What're you doing here, anyway? What happened to the Dragon Balls?"

Goku told him everything that had happened and how he had a whole year before he could hunt for the Dragon Balls again. "So, for the next year, I wanted you to train me," Goku finished.

"You know, my training's awfully tough," Master Roshi said, taking a seat on the couch. "And it'll cost you a pretty penny."

"What's a penny?" Goku asked.

"That's what I thought," the old man said, rolling his eyes.

He looked at the TV again and sighed. "You know, boy, it gets lonely on this island with only my TV and a turtle to keep me company. I'll make you a deal. I'll give you all the training you want if you find me someone to pass the time with."

"Pass the time with?"

"A *wife*, boy-o!" the old master explained. "Well, maybe I should start with a friend. A very good friend who might like me enough to marry me."

"So you want me to find you a friend?" Goku asked.

"Not just any friend. Someone with spunk and beauty," Master Roshi said. "Kinda like your friend Bulma."

"So if I find you a friend like Bulma," Goku said, "you'll train me?"

"I'll train you to be as powerful as you can be," Master Roshi said.

That was all Goku needed to hear. "Kinto'un!" he called, racing outside. His magic cloud zoomed down from the sky.

"I'm counting on you to find me someone special, boy!" Master Roshi called, and Goku zoomed out of sight.

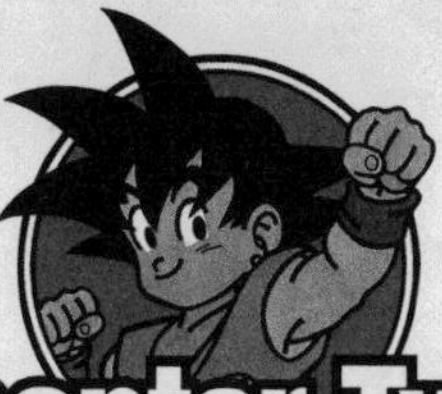

Chapter Two

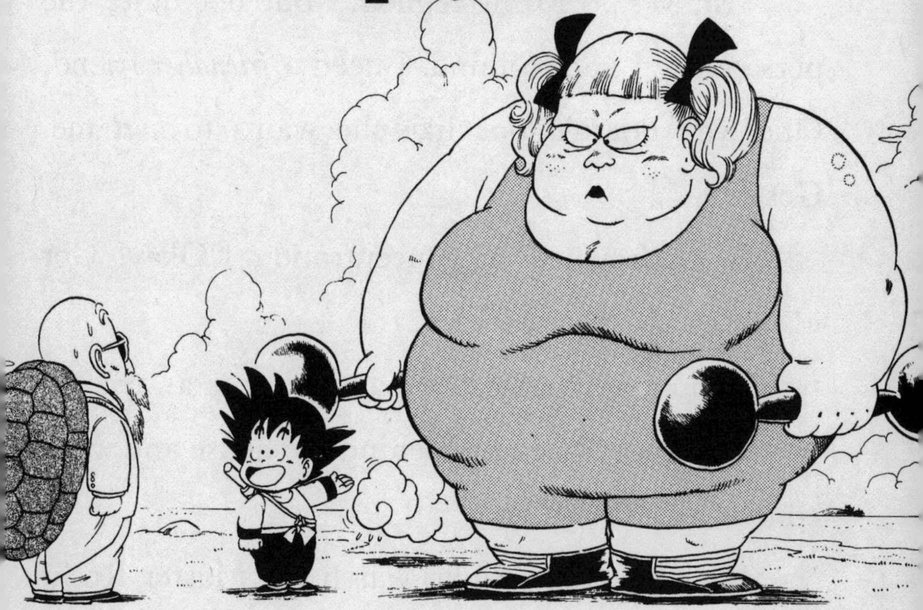

"Okay, old timer! I'm back!"

"That was fast," the old man muttered as he rushed out of his house.

Standing next to Goku was a very angry-looking woman with a scowl that made the turtle master shake in his shell.

"Um...Goku? Can I talk to you for a moment?"

"She's got a lot of personality!" Goku grinned as Roshi rushed him away.

"Er, yes..." Roshi replied. "But not quite the personality I had in mind. I need a *friendlier* friend. One who doesn't look like she wants to *hurt* me. Get it?"

Goku frowned in concentration. "Okay! Got it!"

He jumped on his cloud and zoomed away.

This time Roshi hid behind the house and waited for Goku to return.

Moments later, Goku was back. Master Roshi peeked nervously from his hiding place. Sitting on Goku's cloud he saw a woman with a very friendly smile.

"Hi!" she waved.

"Hello!" Roshi replied, beaming. From the corner of his mouth he whispered, "Now this is more like it, Goku!"

14

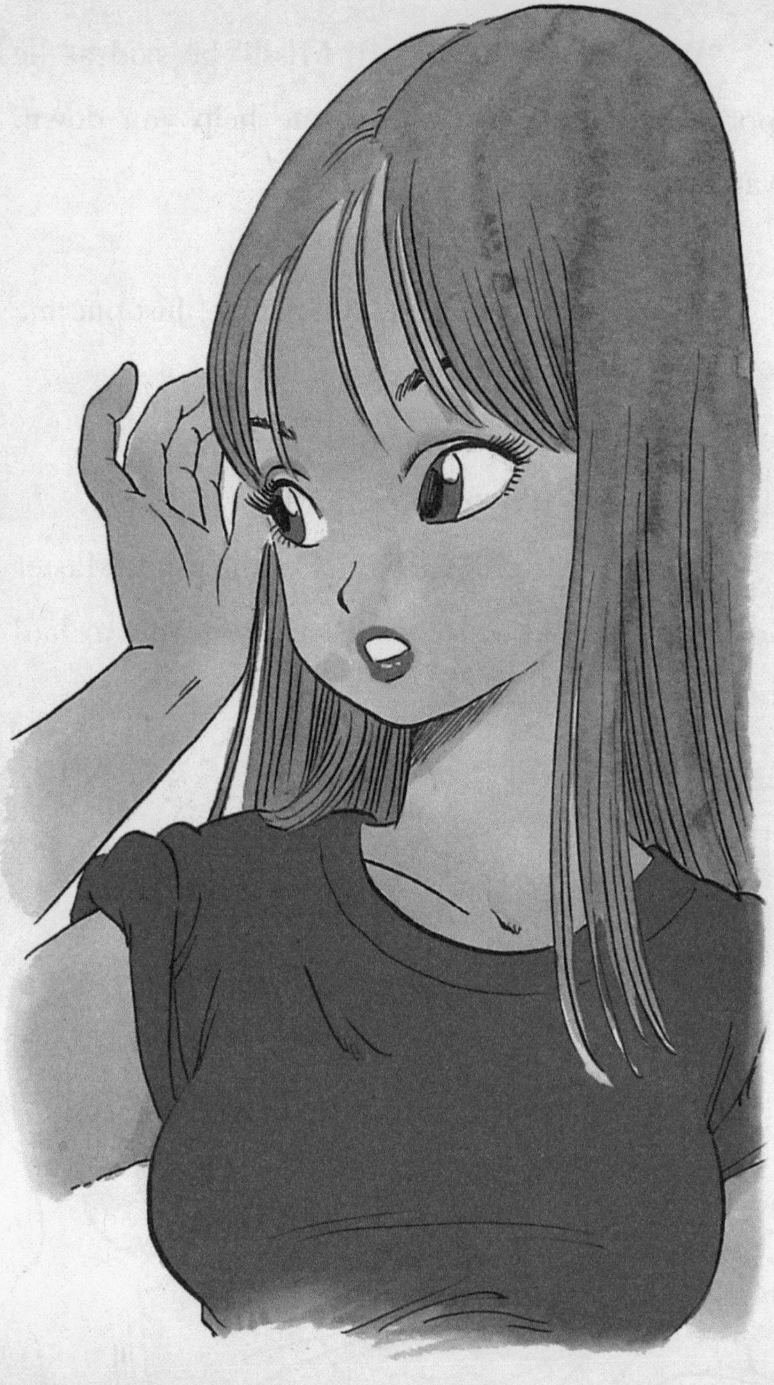

"Welcome to my island, Miss!" he said as he approached the cloud. "Let me help you down. Watch your step."

"Step?" she asked.

Master Roshi frowned. "Of course! Just put one leg over the edge and—"

"Leg?" the woman giggled.

"What's so funny?" Roshi frowned.

As the magic cloud lowered to the sand, Master Roshi understood. Instead of legs, the woman had scales and a tail!

"A *mermaid*?!" Roshi sputtered. "You're a *mermaid*?!"

The mermaid laughed again, then flipped off the cloud and into the sea.

The old master stared after her for a moment, then turned to Goku.

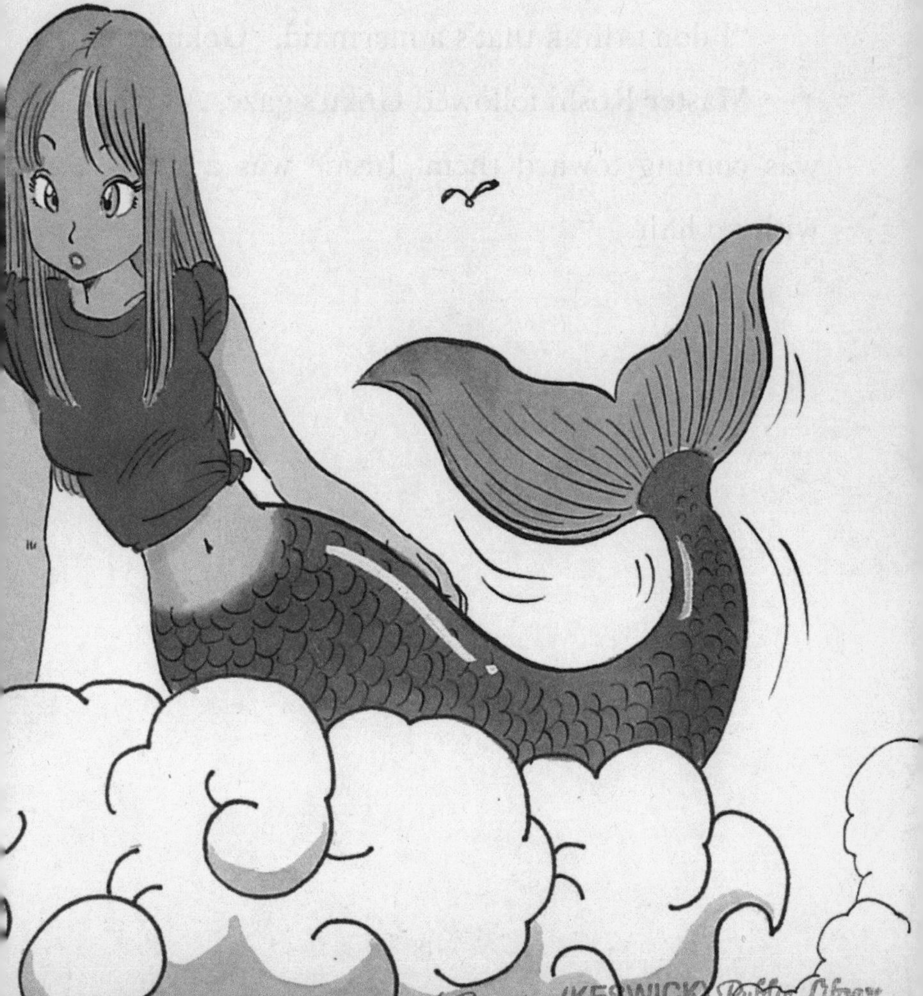

"Okay, listen. Do you want me to train you or not?"

But Goku didn't answer. He just gazed at the water.

"Will you forget about that mermaid and pay attention?" the hermit snapped.

"I don't think that's a mermaid," Goku said.

Master Roshi followed Goku's gaze. A tiny boat was coming toward them. Inside was a small boy with no hair.

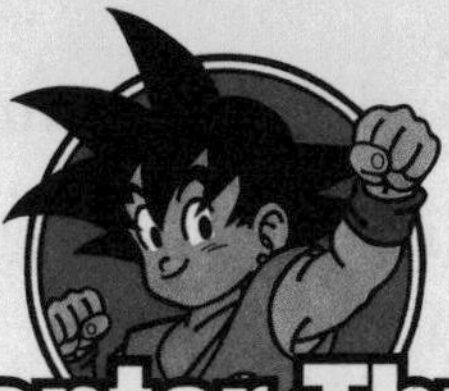

Chapter Three

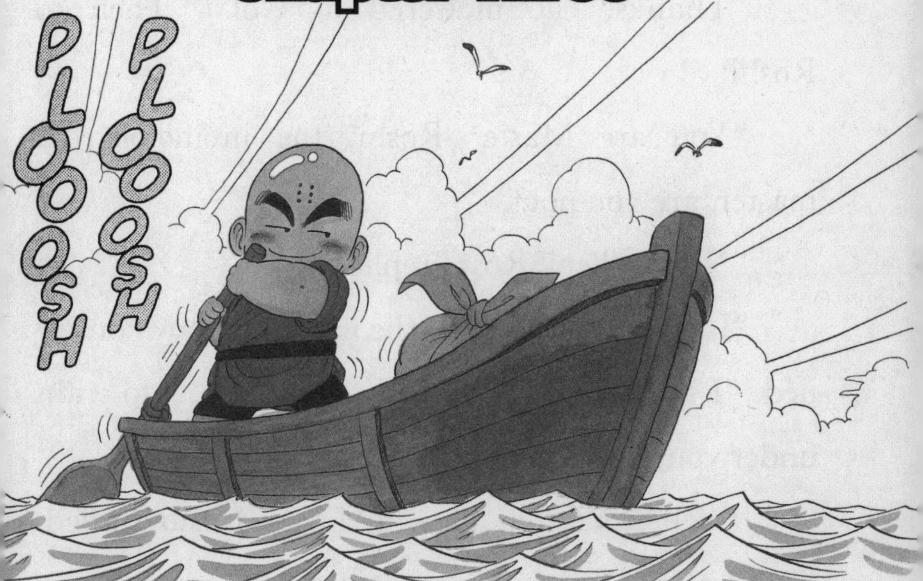
PLOOOOSH
PLOOOOSH

The boat drifted to a stop just offshore. The hairless boy looked at Master Roshi and smirked. Then he cried, "HAYAAAH!" and flung his body into the air. He somersaulted toward the shore and FOOMP! landed headfirst in the sand.

"*Now* what?" Master Roshi sighed. "Pull him out, Goku."

Goku pulled and the boy came free with a sandy POP. He dusted himself off and stood up as tall as he could, which wasn't very tall at all.

"Thanks," he muttered to Goku. Then to Roshi:

"You are Master Roshi, the invincible old master, are you not?"

"None other," Roshi replied.

"I have traveled from the east!" the boy continued. "I am called Krillin. My only wish is to train under you, most honorable Master!"

"Well, isn't that nice?" Master Roshi smiled. "But I already have one student, and one is enough. Have a nice trip home!"

"Wait!" Krillin cried. "I will do anything to win the favor of the great master!"

"*Anything*?" Master Roshi replied. He thought for a moment. "Do you think you could find me a wife? A *human* one?" he said, looking sharply at Goku.

"And not one with too much personality,"

Goku said.

Krillin looked sharply at Goku. "Who are *you*?"

"I'm Son Goku!" Goku replied. "And the turtle guy's gonna train me!"

Krillin looked him up and down. "You don't look like you have the stomach for training."

"Oh, I've got plenty of stomach." Goku grinned.

"Are you trying to be funny?"

"Nah, you're the funny one," Goku said. "Your head looks like a lightbulb!"

"How dare you?!" Krillin roared. "Anyone who's serious about martial arts shaves his head! Look at Master Roshi!"

"Actually," said Master Roshi, "I'm just bald."

Krillin blushed bright red.

"But I'll agree to train you," added the master, "if you'll help Goku find me a wife."

"Done!" Krillin cried.

"All right then. Get going," said the old master. "And no fish this time!"

Goku jumped onto Kinto'un. Krillin watched him suspiciously. "You can...ride a *cloud*?"

"It's really fun!" Goku said. "Come on!"

"Okay, then," Krillin said. "Here I–"

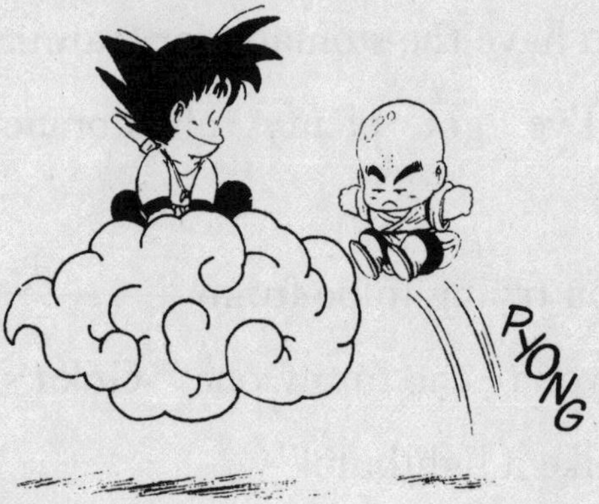
PYONG

FOOMP!

Krillin dropped straight through the cloud and landed headfirst in the sand.

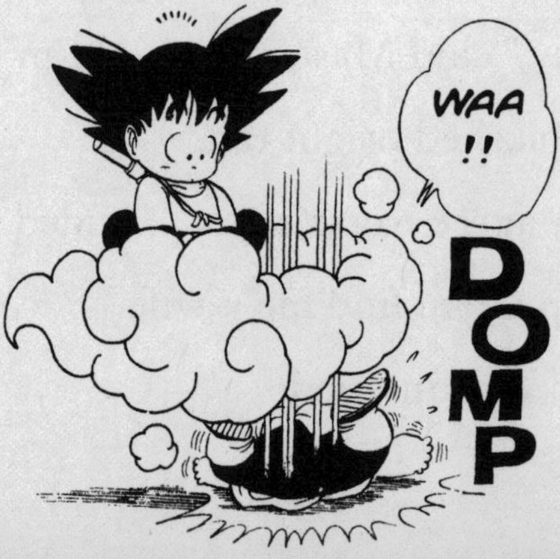
WAA !!
DOMP

"Is this a trick?!" he sputtered, pulling himself free.

"Interesting," Master Roshi said. "The cloud can only be ridden by those with a pure heart! You can't ride it, which must mean...you've come here with impure intentions!"

"No way!" Krillin gasped. "All I want is to be a great martial arts master...so I can be more popular with girls!"

Master Roshi just looked at him. "We may need to discuss your definition of 'pure.'"

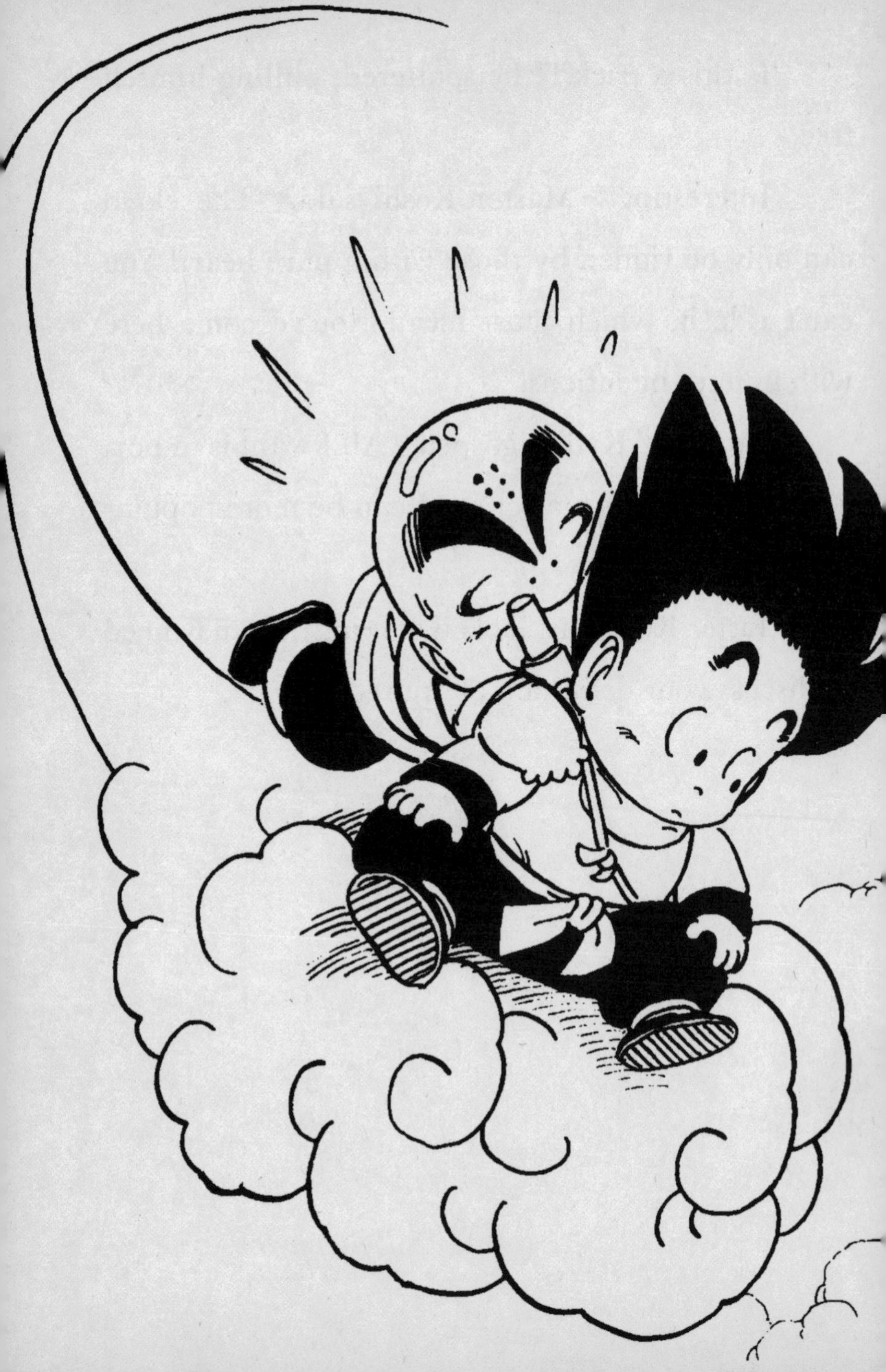

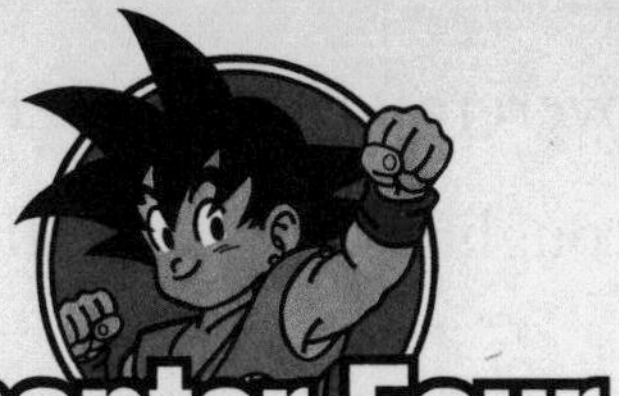

Chapter Four

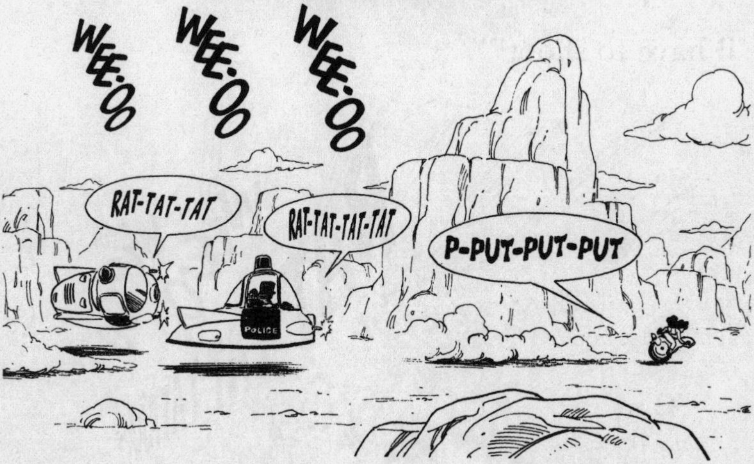
WEE-OO
WEE-OO
WEE-OO
P-PUT-PUT-PUT
RAT-TAT-TAT-TAT
RAT-TAT-TAT
POLICE

Goku steered his magic cloud across the sea while Krillin hung on for dear life.

"Fly a little lower and slower, would you?!" Krillin screamed. "If I lose my grip I'm a goner!"

"It's not my fault your heart isn't pure!" Goku yelled back.

"Why you–" Krillin growled, but he was cut short by the sound of sirens. Below them a girl on a one-wheeled motorbike raced out of the city.

Two police hovercraft chased after her, sirens screaming. Goku brought Kinto'un a little lower to get a closer look.

"Stop!" yelled one of the policemen. "Stop or we'll have to shoot!"

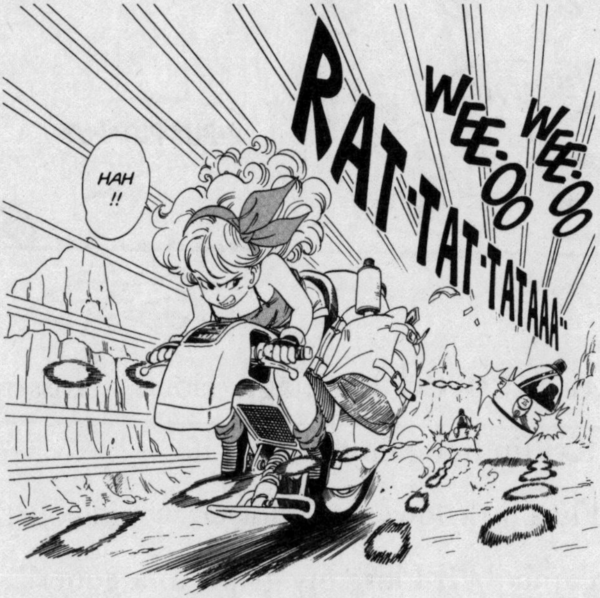
HAH !!
RAT-TAT-TAT-TATAAA
WEE-OO WEE-OO

The girl looked back at them and laughed. The police fired their handguns and engaged the weapons mounted on the front of their vehicles.

The girl reached into her bag and pulled out a grenade. With a smirk, she threw it behind her.

"Look out!" one of the policemen screamed. He turned his car frantically, but it was no use. The grenade exploded, flipping the hovercraft upside down. Now there was only one police car left.

The girl laughed. She turned her bike sharply and zoomed up the side of a steep cliff. When she reached the top, she flew over the edge, then landed hard in a narrow ravine.

"There she is!" cried the cops.

The girl turned to look behind her. A strand of her hair blew across her face and tickled her nose.

"ARGH!" she screamed. "Not now!" But there was nothing she could do.

"Ah..." she wheezed. "Ah...AH-CHOO!"

The force of her sneeze sent her flying backwards off her bike. She sat on the ground for a moment, dazed.

"Wha—what happened?" she asked the policemen who had now gotten out of their car and were coming toward her with handcuffs. She wasn't quite

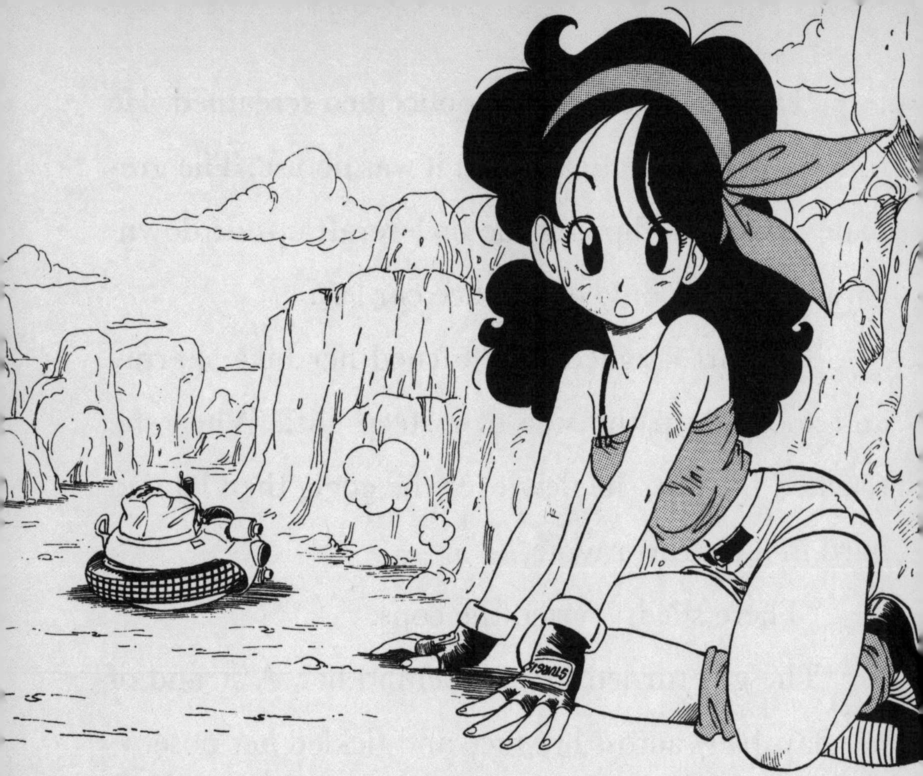
STURGIS

the girl she had been a moment ago. Instead of blonde, this girl's hair was dark. Instead of being tough and fearless, this girl looked small and scared.

"What do you mean, 'what happened'?" said one of the officers, inching closer. "We've been chasing you for miles. And now you're under arrest!"

"Under arrest?" the girl cried. "I don't understand! Please! Somebody help me!"

At that moment Goku and Krillin flew over the

scene. "We've got to help her!" Goku cried.

"Help her how?!" Krillin wailed. "We're not even martial arts masters yet! And they've got guns! This is dangerous!"

"Let's do it!" Goku said. And down he jumped—with Krillin holding on tight and screaming the whole way.

"Wha—?!" Gasped one of the policemen when they landed. "Who the heck are you?"

"We're here to rescue that girl!" Goku replied.

"Not me!" Krillin screamed, letting go of Goku and dashing behind a rock. "And just so you know, I don't even know this kid."

"So you wanna play hero?" one of the officers said, turning his gun on Goku. "Just stay out of our way or we'll arrest you too."

With a quick chop to the officer's wrist, Goku knocked the gun out of his hand. Before the officer could react, Goku landed a swift kick and knocked him out cold. Then Goku bounded into the air and

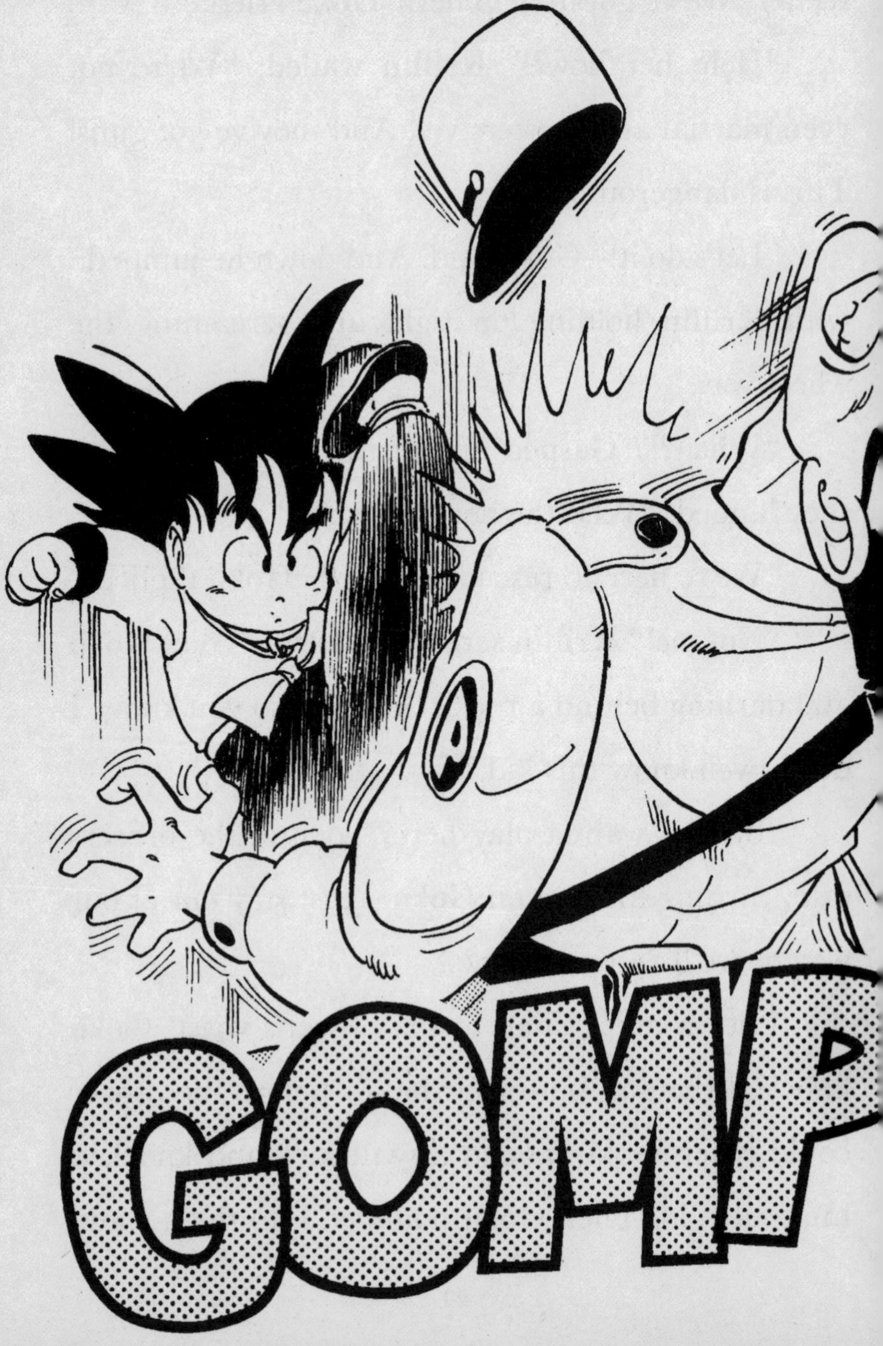
GOMP

turned toward the second officer. He flipped toward the cop and–GONK!–knocked him out with a powerful headbutt.

From his hiding place, Krillin stared in amazement.

The dark-haired girl rushed toward Goku. "Thank you, thank you!" she cried. "How can I ever repay your kindness?"

Krillin rushed from his hiding place. "Oh, please!" he said. "It was no trouble at all!"

"Hey, Krillin," Goku said looking at the girl. "Is she beautiful?"

"And friendly!" Krillin nodded. "And charming!"

"Does she look like she might hurt the Turtle Guy?"

"Not a chance."

A minute later, the girl was sitting on the cloud behind Goku, and they were zooming back across the ocean.

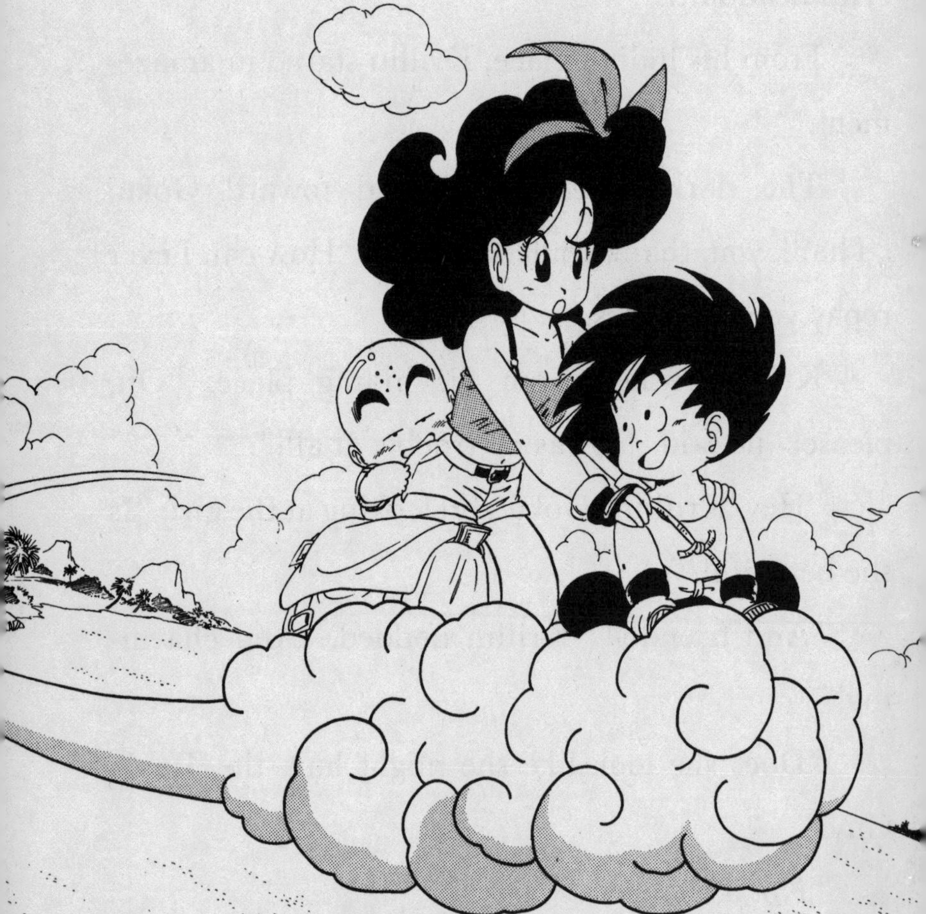

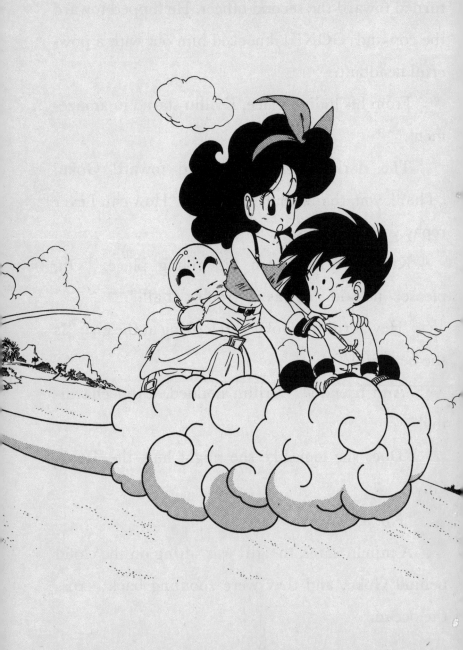

Chapter Five

"Welcome to Turtle Island, my dear," Master Roshi said when they arrived. "May I ask your name?"

"Lunch!" the girl said.

"Soon, very soon!" the master said. "But what's your name?"

"*Lunch*," the girl said. "That *is* my name. And I'd be very grateful if I could stay here for a little while...if it's not too much trouble..."

"No trouble at all!"

"Well, I think I should warn you..." Lunch started to say.

"Warnings can wait!" laughed the master. "Step inside and I'll give you the tour of the humble but legendary home of the humble but legendary Master...*argh*!"

"Master Argh?" Lunch asked.

"A bee!" the master yelled, swatting at a flying bug with his walking stick. "Shoo! Shoo!"

The bee buzzed away from him and flew right under Lunch's nose.

"Oh no," she moaned. "Run!"

The she started to wheeze.

"Nonsense!" chuckled Master Roshi. "It's just a bee!"

"No, no..." Lunch wheezed. The sneeze was building. "When...I...I...I...AH-CHOO!"

Suddenly sweet, dark-haired Lunch was gone. In her place stood the blonde girl on the motorbike. And she was not happy.

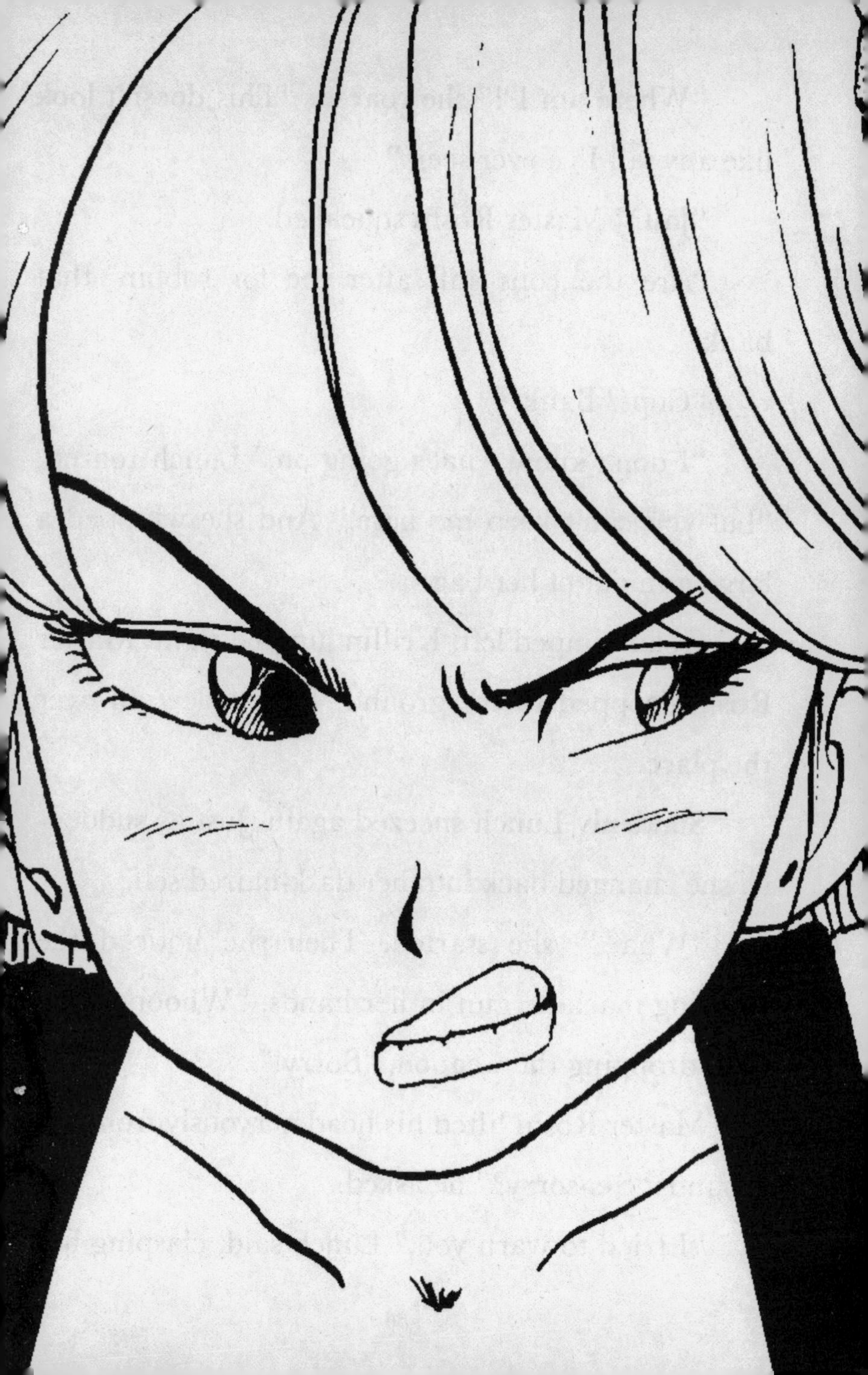

"Where am I?!" she roared. "This doesn't look like any jail I've ever seen."

"Jail?" Master Roshi squeaked.

"Are the cops still after me for robbin' that bank?"

"Cops? Bank?"

"I don't know what's going on," Lunch roared, "but you can't keep me here!" And she whipped a large gun out of her bag.

Goku jumped left. Krillin jumped right. Master Roshi dropped to the ground. Bullets flew all over the place.

Suddenly Lunch sneezed again. Just as suddenly, she changed back into her dark-haired self.

"Wha–?" she started. Then she noticed the smoking machine gun in her hands. "Whoops!" she said, dropping the weapon. "Sorry!"

Master Roshi lifted his head nervously from the ground. "S-s-sorry?" he asked.

"I tried to warn you," Lunch said, clasping her

hands in front of her like a little girl. "Whenever I sneeze I...you know...change."

"No kidding!" yelled Krillin.

"Yeah," Lunch laughed. "I just hope I didn't cause too much trouble."

"Oh, n-n-no," Master Roshi said, standing up on shaking legs. "N-n-no trouble at all."

"C-c-can we take her back now?" Krillin whispered.

"You know what?" the old master said with a nervous laugh. "I kinda like her. We'll just have to keep her from sneezing."

"This is gonna be great," Krillin said, rolling his eyes.

"Can we start training now?" Goku asked.

"Yes," said Master Roshi. "But first we need to move to a bigger island."

He packed his small house into one Hoi-Poi capsule and–BAM!–produced a motorboat from another. "Let's roll!"

Chapter Six

ANCHORS AWEIGH!!

BWOOO---N

"This looks like a good spot," Roshi said as he steered the boat ashore. The new island was much larger than his old home. It had a town at one end and tall mountains in the middle, but it was mostly covered in forest. A perfect place to train.

The old master set up his house on the beach while Goku and Krillin gathered food in the jungle.

Lunch volunteered to make dinner (and Master Roshi made sure there was no pepper or anything else that might make her sneeze).

As the sun began to set, Master Roshi took his new students to a field. It was finally time to begin.

"Krillin, have you had any martial arts training?" the master asked.

"Yes!" Krillin replied. "I've trained for eight years."

"Let's see what you've got. It is exactly 100 meters from here to that tree," Roshi continued. "How fast can you run it?"

"*Fast*," Krillin smirked. "I guarantee you'll never see anybody faster than me!"

"Alright then," the master laughed. "On your mark...get set...go!" And Krillin zoomed to the tree.

"Unbelievable!" the master said, looking at his stopwatch. "What a feat! And what *feet*! Only 10.4 seconds!"

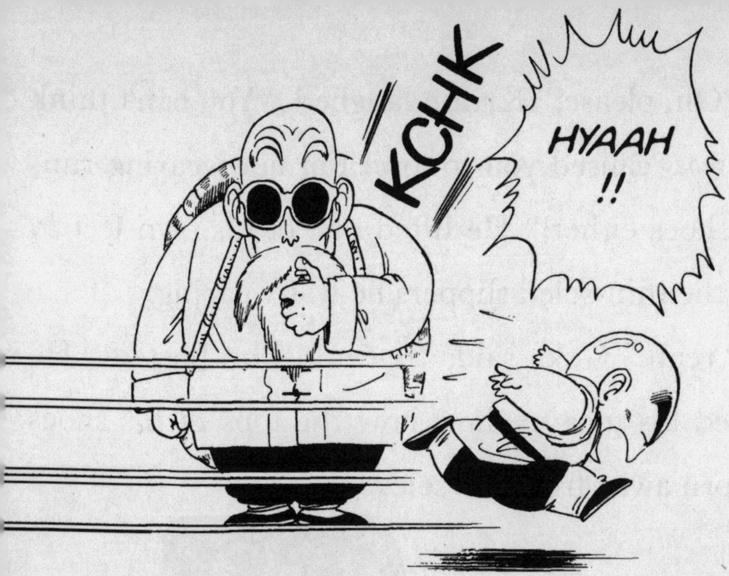
KCHK
HYAAH !!

"Must be a little rusty," Krillin huffed. "My personal best is 10.1, but," he smiled, "10.4 isn't too bad."

Then it was Goku's turn.

"Ready? Set! Go!" Roshi called. Goku took off.

"Impressive," Master Roshi said. "Eleven seconds. Not as fast as Krillin, but still fast."

Krillin chuckled. "Well, it's not really fair to compare, is it? He has his own strengths, I'm sure."

"I'm sure," Roshi chuckled.

"Hey, old timer," Goku said, walking back toward them. "Can I change my shoes and try again?"

"Oh, please!" Krillin laughed. "You can't think your *shoes* caused you to lose! I'm not wearing running shoes either!" He lifted one of his own feet to show the thin-soled slippers he was wearing.

"Yeah," Goku said, "but mine are busted!" He wiggled his toes to show how the tops of his shoes had torn away from the soles.

FLOP FLOP

Krillin's mouth dropped open.

"I can't believe it," Master Roshi muttered as he pulled the shoes off Krillin's feet.

"B-but, Master!" Krillin protested. But Roshi had already handed Krillin's shoes to Goku.

"Oh yeah!" Goku cried, jumping up and down. "Much better! I'm ready!"

"Go!" Roshi cried.

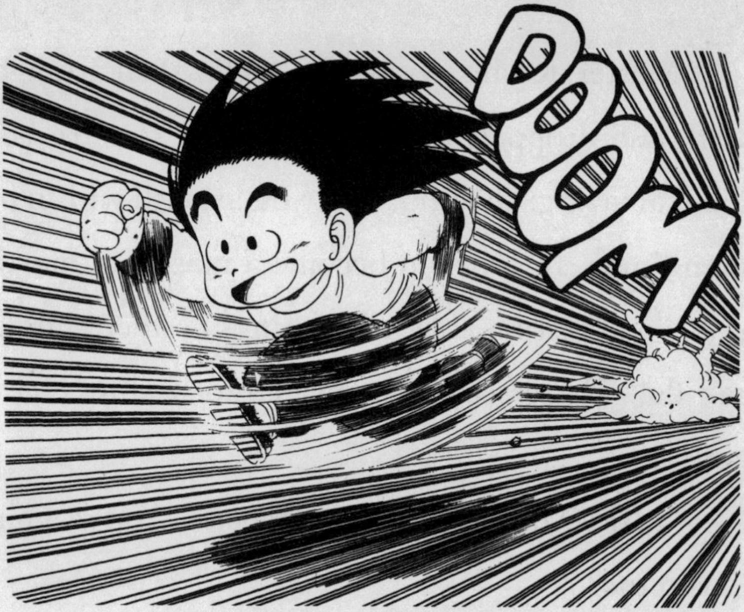
DOOOM

Goku ran. "Done!" he cried when he had reached the tree. Master Roshi looked at his stopwatch. "Eight...point...five...seconds," he breathed.

"Is that fast?" Goku asked eagerly.

"The record, as far as I know," Master Roshi replied, "is 9.6 seconds."

Goku looked disappointed. "You mean that Record guy got more than me?"

"It's not fair!" Krillin cried, yanking his shoes off Goku's feet. "No one that stupid should be that fast!"

Master Roshi swung the turtle shell from his back and dropped it to the ground. "You are both quite amazing," he said, "but you are still within human limits. In order to become a master of martial arts, you must be able to do things no mere human can do!" He tossed his stopwatch to Krillin. "Time me."

"M-M-Master," Krillin gasped. "You're going to run too?"

"But you're so old!" Goku said.

The master laid his walking stick on the ground and said, "Whenever you're ready, Krillin."

"G-g-get ready," Krillin said, looking at the stopwatch. "S-s-set...**GO!**"

One moment Krillin and Goku saw the master in his runner's stance. The next moment they saw only a blur. And suddenly the master was standing under the tree. "How long was that?" he called.

"*5.6 seconds!*" Krillin gasped.

"Not bad for an old codger, eh?" the old master

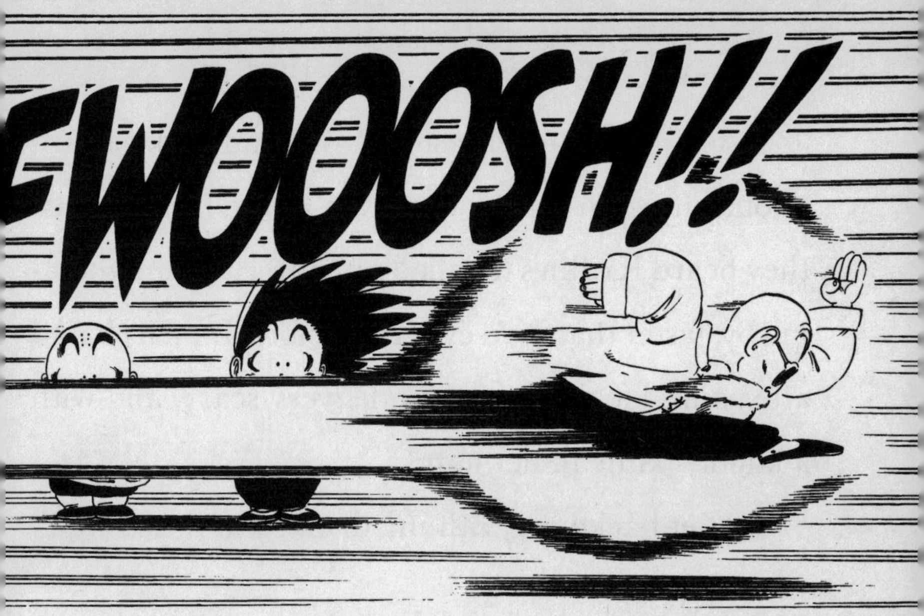
WOOOSH!!

asked, walking slowly back and picking up his walking stick. "And with your youth and strength, you should be able to run this in five seconds! But to do so, you must submit to the most rigorous training imaginable! Are you willing?"

"Yes, Master!" said Krillin and Goku at the same time.

"Excellent," said the master. "But first, I'm thirsty. Which of you wants to go back to the house and get me something to drink?"

"I will, I will!" Krillin yelled first, and he

raced away.

A minute later, Master Roshi and Goku heard a loud sneeze from the direction of the house. Then they heard Krillin's terrified scream. He came zooming by, faster than he'd ever run before. Lunch chased after him, looking very blonde, very scary, and with a kitchen knife in her hand.

"Get back here with my drink, you little thief!" she screamed.

"Heeeeeeeeeeeelp!" Krillin yelled.

"See?" called Master Roshi as they ran by. "Now *that's* fast!"

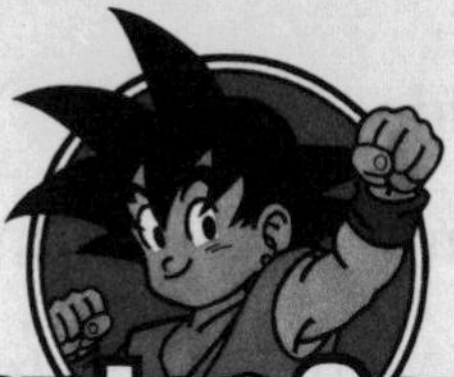

Chapter Seven

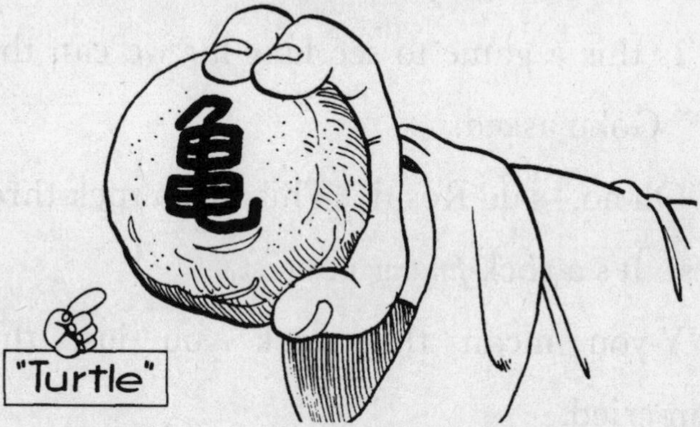
亀
"Turtle"

By now the sun was low in the sky. "Tomorrow we'll begin the real training," Master Roshi said. "But tonight there's a delicious dinner waiting for us."

"Yes!" Goku cried.

Roshi picked up a rock and wrote the Japanese character for "turtle" on it.

"But first," he said thoughtfully, "one last test for today. Look closely at this rock." The master held it out for his students to see. "Have you studied it?"

The boys nodded.

"Good." Then with all his might, Roshi heaved the rock off a cliff. "Ho, ho! Quite a distance!" Roshi laughed, watching the rock fall.

"Is this a game to see how far we can throw a rock?" Goku asked.

"Oh no," said Roshi. "This isn't a rock-throwing contest. It's a rock-*finding* contest."

"Y-you mean that rock you just threw?" Krillin cried.

"Finding that rock will require not only stamina and speed," Roshi replied, "but great mental concentration. Whoever brings it back to me is the winner. And only the winner...gets dinner!" As if that weren't hard enough, he added, "In fact, if neither of you has found the rock in thirty minutes...*neither* of you gets dinner!"

Both boys raced for the edge of the cliff. "They're aren't any footholds!" Krillin cried, looking down. "We'll have to go arou–"

But Goku jumped over the edge of the cliff without a word. On the way down he caught a tree limb to break his fall. Unfortunately, all he did was break it in half. Goku landed with a mighty thud, but he didn't let that stop him. "Remember dinner, remember dinner!" he said to himself, and started sorting through the rocks at the base of the cliff.

Is this kid human? Krillin thought as he watched from above. *Whatever he is, he's way ahead of me, so I guess I'd better—*

Krillin was just about to leap when he stopped.

Wait. He thought. *There's no way anyone can find that rock in under thirty minutes. There must be another way.*

Meanwhile, Goku searched everywhere for the rock. He sniffed the air. *I can smell the Turtle Guy's scent!* he thought. *That rock's got to be around here somewhere!*

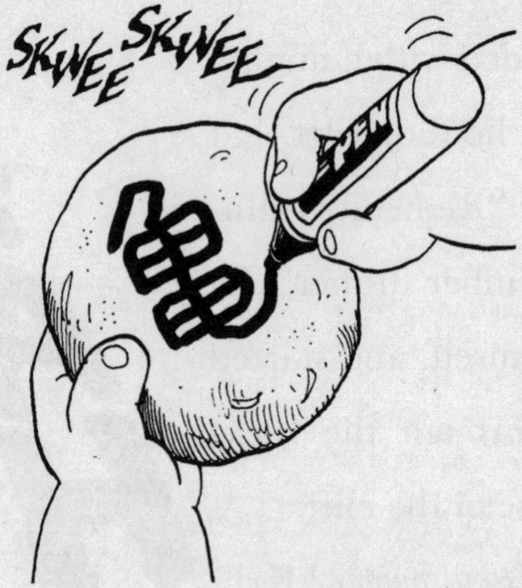
SKWEE SKWEE
PEN

Krillin, on the other hand, had given up looking. He'd found a rock similar to the one he and Goku were looking for and wrote the character for "turtle" on it. Then he ran to show Master Roshi.

"I finally found it, Sensei!" he cried, holding the rock out for Roshi to see. The old master grabbed the rock and looked closely. Then he threw it back at Krillin.

"Did you really think you could fool me?! That's not my handwriting! Now back to the forest and find it for real!"

Krillin took off. He had hardly started looking when Goku cried, "I found it! I found it!"

He burst through the bushes with a huge grin on his face and Master Roshi's rock in his hand.

"You found it?" Krillin demanded. "How?"

"I smelled it!" Goku grinned. "The old timer's scent was all over it!"

HEH HEH HEH...

"What are you, a dog?" Krillin grumbled. "I'll bet it's not even the real thing. Lemme see."

As soon as Goku handed him the rock, Krillin snatched it away.

"Sucker!" Krillin yelled, and took off at top speed.

"Hey!" Goku cried. "That's not fair! Get back here!" And he took off after Krillin.

Krillin raced over a rope bridge. When he got to the other side he hacked at the bridge until the ropes

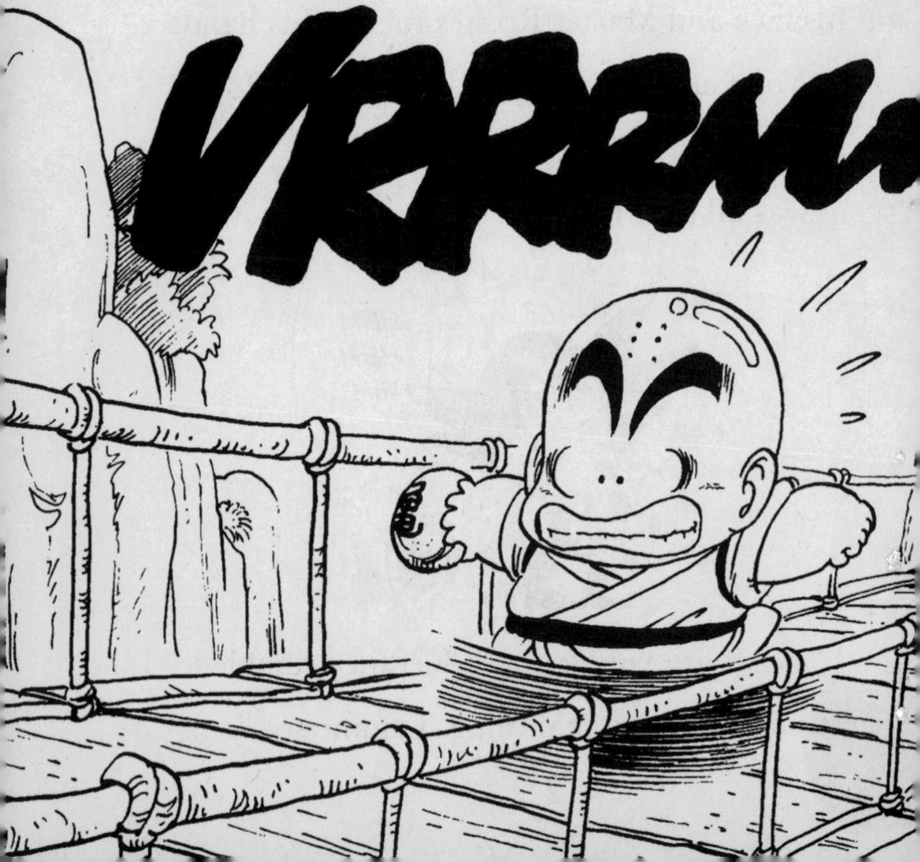
VRRRM

came loose. Goku had only made it halfway across. When the bridge fell, he plummeted with it.

"Yes!" laughed Krillin as he took off at top speed again. He looked over his shoulder and there, not twenty steps behind him, was Goku!

"What?!" Krillin cried. Then he stopped and spun around. "Fine. I can see that the only way to get rid of you is to fight!"

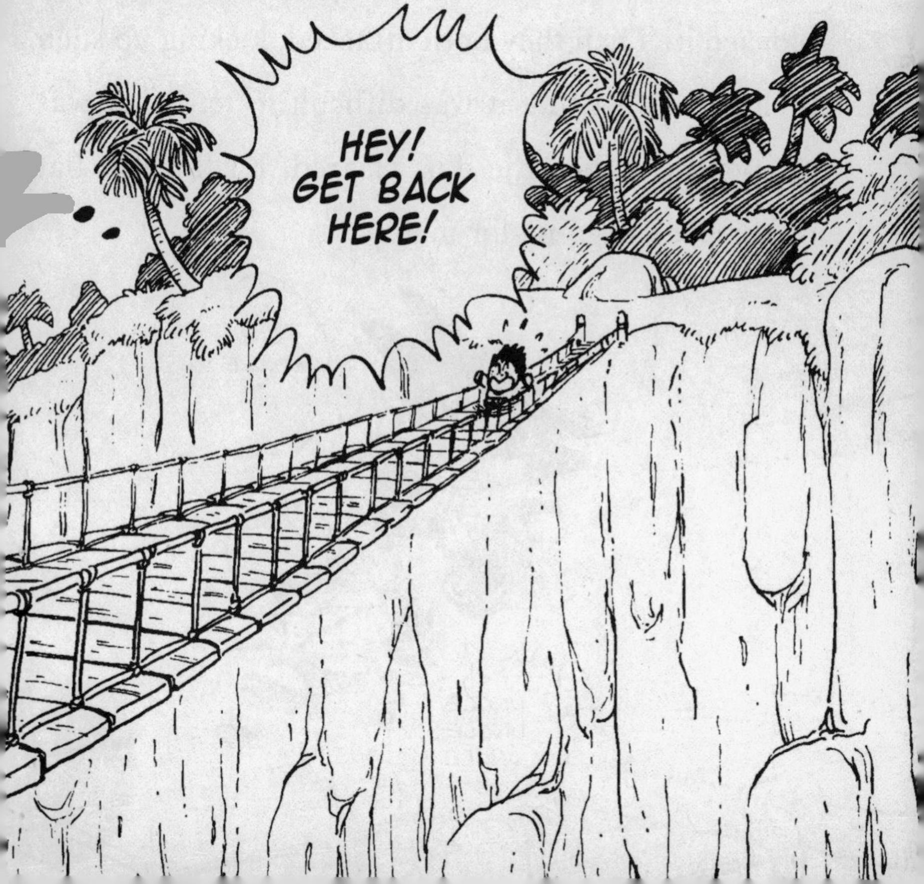
HEY! GET BACK HERE!

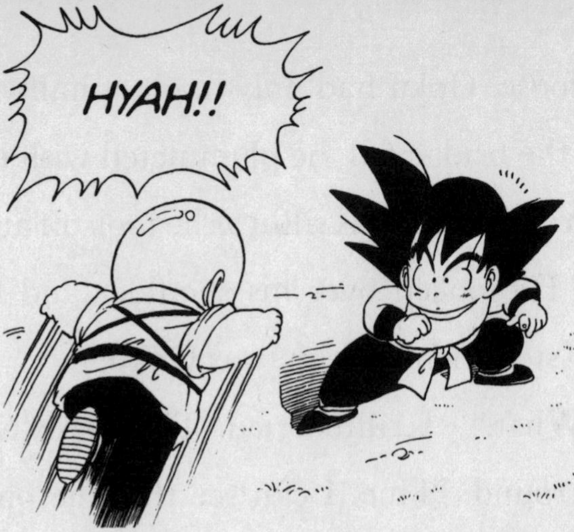
HYAH!!

He leapt at Goku with a flying kick–but Goku blocked it. Then they both attacked, kicking up such a cloud of dust that it was difficult to tell what was happening. When the dust cleared, Krillin was flat on his back begging for mercy.

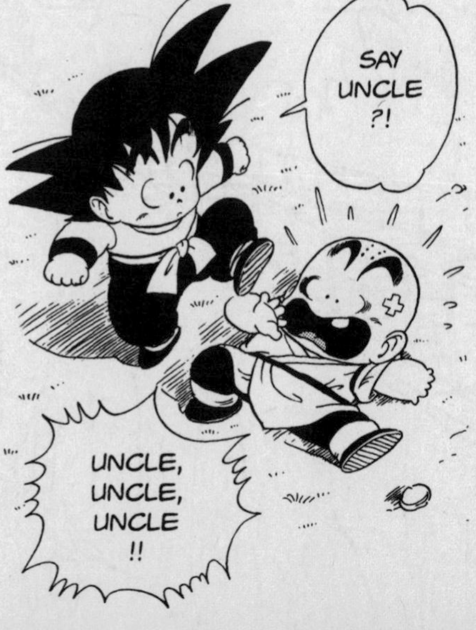
SAY UNCLE ?!
UNCLE, UNCLE, UNCLE !!

"Give me back my rock!" Goku cried.

"Okay...okay..." Krillin panted, reaching inside his shirt for the rock. "Go get it!," he yelled as he threw the rock as far as he could.

Goku ran after it. As soon as he was gone, Krillin started to laugh. He reached into his shirt again and pulled out the rock Goku had found. Goku was chasing after the rock Krillin had used to try to fool Master Roshi.

That night, Goku's stomach growled as he watched Krillin gobble the delicious meal that should have been his.

"Part of learning to fight," Master Roshi said through a mouthful of food, "is learning how to outwit your opponents!"

"But he still cheated!" Goku cried.

"Here's another lesson," the master replied. "Sometimes life isn't fair."

As it turned out, Lunch wasn't much of a cook.

The meal she prepared made everyone sick for three straight days. Everyone, that is, except for Goku.

Chapter Eight

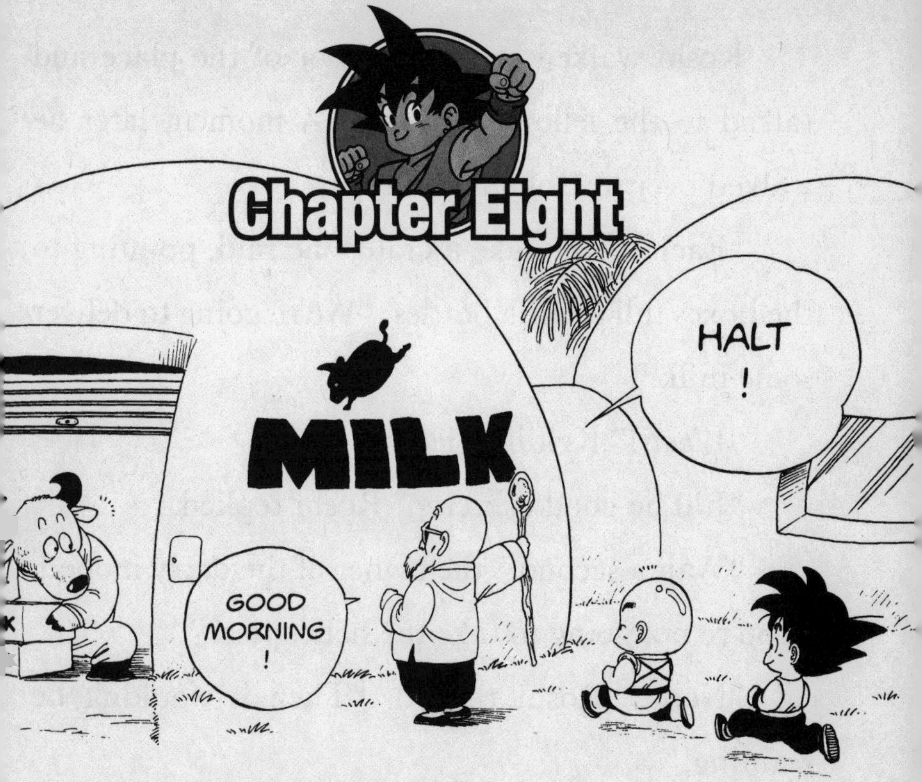
HALT!
MILK
GOOD MORNING!

On the morning everyone recovered, Master Roshi woke the boys at four-thirty. It was time to continue training.

"First some light jogging," he called. "Keep up!" The boys followed behind him. They jogged through the forest and across town until they came to a small building marked "Milk."

"Halt!" cried the master. His students obeyed.

Roshi walked up to the door of the place and talked to the fellow in charge. A moment later he walked over to Goku and Krillin.

"Each of you take a crate," he said, pointing to the boxes full of milk bottles. "We're going to deliver some milk!"

"*What*?!" Krillin cried.

"It'll be good exercise," Roshi replied.

"Wait a second," the owner of the dairy mooed. "You're not going to take the helicopter?"

"Nope," Roshi replied. "Then it wouldn't be training.

"Alright boys, let's go! And let's *skip* to the first house." And so they did.

They took a tree-lined path to the next house, and Master Roshi made them run it in a zigzag pattern. "Come on, Krillin, you're lagging," he called.

Next they carried the crates up a set of steep steps cut into the side of a mountain. Even Goku was out of breath when he reached the top.

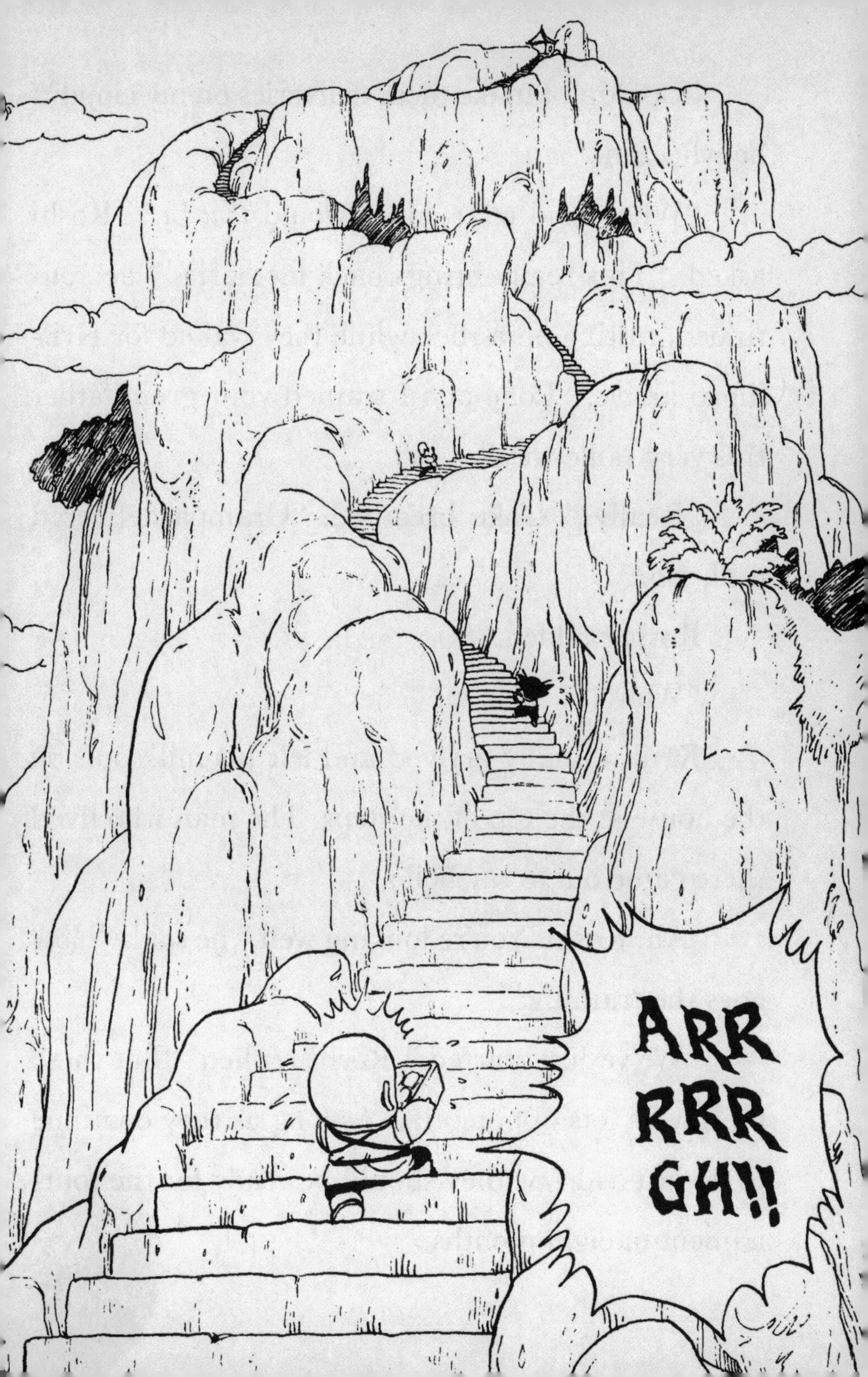
ARR RRR GH!!

"Couldn't I make these deliveries on my cloud?" he wheezed.

"What kind of training would *that* be?" Roshi asked. "This really brings back memories," he continued, resting on a rock while they waited for Krillin to arrive. "Long ago I trained your grandfather this very same way."

"Really?" Goku breathed. "Grampa delivered milk too?"

Roshi nodded.

"Wow."

Krillin finally arrived and left his milk outside the house at the top of the steps. The man who lived there came out to say hello.

"Ah, Roshi. You're looking well," he said. "How goes the training?"

"We've just started," Roshi replied. "But these boys have lots of potential. As long as they continue to do just as I say, they should be ready for the tournament in eight months."

"The Tenka'ichi Budokai?" asked the man. "These must be some special boys."

"Goku, did you hear that?" Krillin whispered. "Master Roshi is training us to compete in the 'Strongest Under the Heavens'!"

"What's that?"

"It's a tournament where the most powerful fighters from all over the world compete for the ultimate title: *Strongest Under the Heavens*!"

"Sounds awesome!" Goku cried.

"Master Roshi," Krillin called, "do you really think we'll be able to enter?"

"If you train hard," the master replied. "However, the goal is not to win. Just qualifying will be sufficient."

"Yeah, just to compete would be amazing!" Krillin breathed.

"There's gonna be lots of strong guys, right?" Goku asked excitedly.

"That milk is getting warm, boys," Master Roshi

laughed. "Let's go."

For the rest of the morning Krillin and Goku trained hard. For balance, they carried their milk crates over a narrow log that crossed a deep ravine. For strength, they carried their crates through quicksand and against the current of a raging river. For speed they ran from a rampaging dinosaur, though Krillin wasn't quite sure that was an intentional part of the training.

Finally, they had delivered all of the milk. "Congratulations, boys!" Master Roshi beamed.

"We survived!" Krillin wheezed.

"You've survived your early morning routine," Roshi smiled. "Now it's time to really get the day started!"

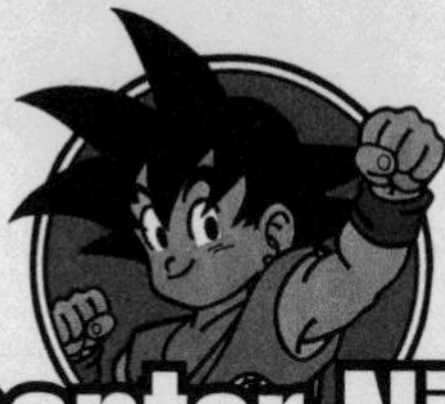

Chapter Nine

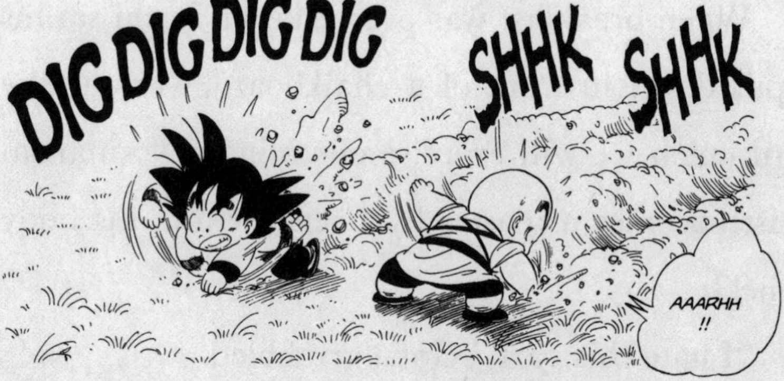
SHHK SHHK
AAARHH !!
DIG DIG DIG DIG

"First, you'll plow these fields," Master Roshi said, pointing to a farm that stretched far and wide in all directions.

"These fields are huge!" Krillin whined. But he picked up a hoe and got to work.

"What're you doing?" Master Roshi asked. "No tools! You'll plow these fields with your bare hands."

Goku and Krillin got to work while Roshi watched. Finally, filthy and panting, the boys were finished.

"What took you so long?" Roshi asked. "Tomorrow's fields will be much bigger and you'll have to go much faster. But before we worry about tomorrow, let's have breakfast."

When breakfast was over, Master Roshi sat his pupils down in front of a chalkboard. "From now until lunch we will exercise our minds. No martial artist becomes a master by strengthening his body alone!"

"I hate this part," Goku grumbled.

After lunch, it was time for a nap. "Move well, study well, play well, eat well," Roshi sighed from his hammock. "That is the Turtle Master way."

When naptime was over, Goku was ready for something different.

"Old timer," he said. "When are you gonna teach us some moves?"

"What?!" Roshi roared. "You've just started your training! You're hardly strong enough to start learning moves! Come here." He led them to a huge boulder that was twice his height and three times as wide.

“I’ll teach you some moves as soon as you’re strong enough to move this rock.”

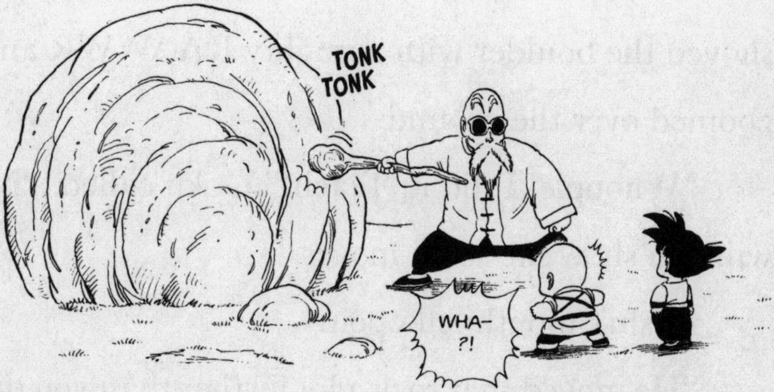
TONK
TONK
WHA-
?!

“Impossible!” Krillin cried. “No one can move a boulder that size!”

“Oh no?” Master Roshi chuckled. “Hold this.” He handed Krillin his cane and put his hands on the boulder. Then he pushed with all his might. Very slowly, the boulder moved.

“Now do you understand?” Roshi panted. “If you train hard, one day you’ll be able to move this rock, too.”

"Lemme try that," said Goku as he stepped up to the boulder. He pushed, but the stone didn't move.

"You see?" the master chuckled. "You have a long way to go!"

"I guess I gotta push hard," Goku said. He shoved the boulder with a mighty RAAWWR and it zoomed over the ground.

"Whoopie! I did it, Teach!" Goku called. "Now will you show me some moves?"

Roshi's mouth fell open.

"He moved that rock a lot farther than you did," Krillin whispered.

Master Roshi just stared. Then he forced himself to laugh. "Silly me!" he said. "That-that's not the right rock. This-*this* is the boulder I meant." And he led them to a rock that might as well have been a small mountain.

"Awk!" Goku yelled. "We've gotta be strong enough to push *that*?" He leaned against it but it wouldn't budge.

"See-see!" the turtle master said with some relief. "You need more training. Much, much more."

"Can you move it, old timer?" Goku asked.

"Of course."

"Show us! Show us!" Krillin cried eagerly.

Master Roshi looked at the rock.

"Let's not get distracted," he said. "Training! Let's get back to our training!

"See this river? I want you to swim ten laps across it. Go!"

"Finally something easy," Krillin sighed.

"Watch out for the shark!" Master Roshi called.

When their laps were done, Master Roshi prepared his students for one last exercise. "Hold still," he said, as he tied ropes around their waists.

"What's this for?" Goku asked.

"This exercise will test your reflexes," the master replied as he tied the other ends of the ropes around the trunk of a nearby tree.

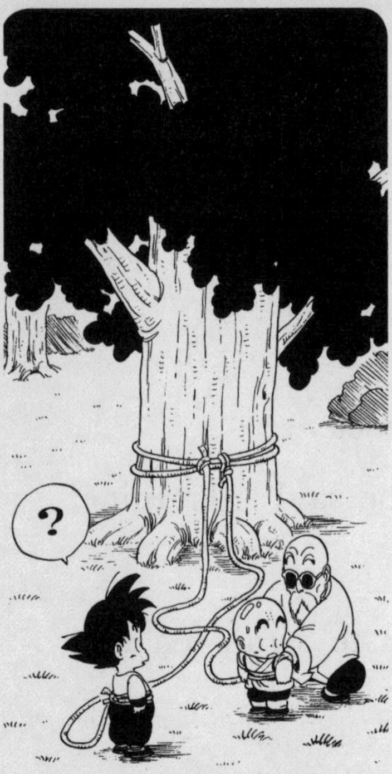
?

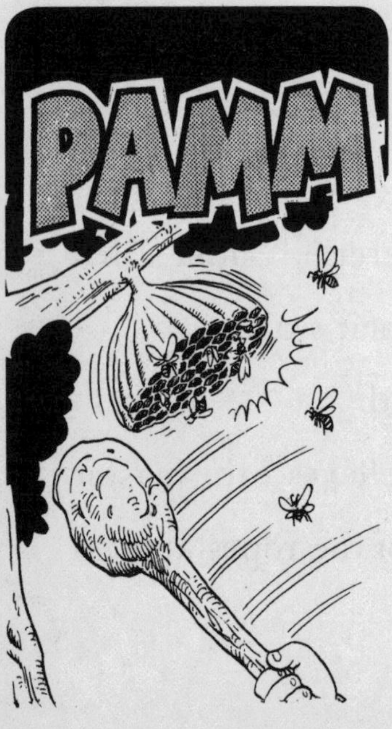
PAMM

"Now. The point here is to dodge your enemies' attacks, but you can only move as much as these ropes will allow."

"Enemy?" Goku asked.

"Attacks?" Krillin cried.

"That's right," Roshi whispered as he tiptoed toward the tree. "Hmm..." he said, looking through the branches. "I know I saw one somewhere..."

"What're you looking for?" Krillin asked.

"This!" Roshi cried, and he whapped a wasps' nest with the head of his cane. Then he took off running as fast as he could, leaving Krillin and Goku to fend for themselves against the angry swarm.

"Step lively!" Roshi called from a safe distance away. "You don't want to get stung!"

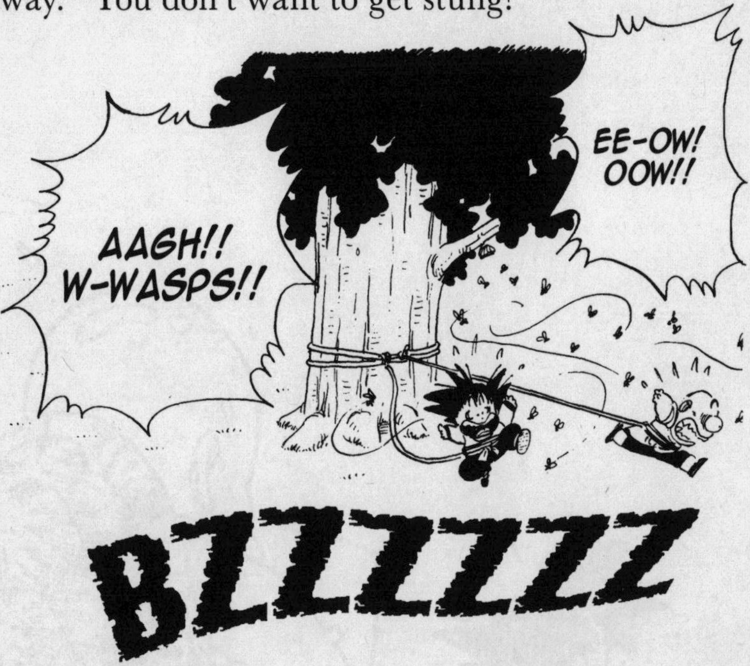
EE-OW! OOW!!
AAGH!! W-WASPS!!
BZZZZZZ

Finally the day was done and it was time to go home.

"Master," Krillin asked as they walked, "will training be like this every day?"

"Of course not," Roshi replied. "Today was just a warm-up. For the next eight months, you'll be doing the exact same exericses...with a forty-pound tortoise shell on your back!"

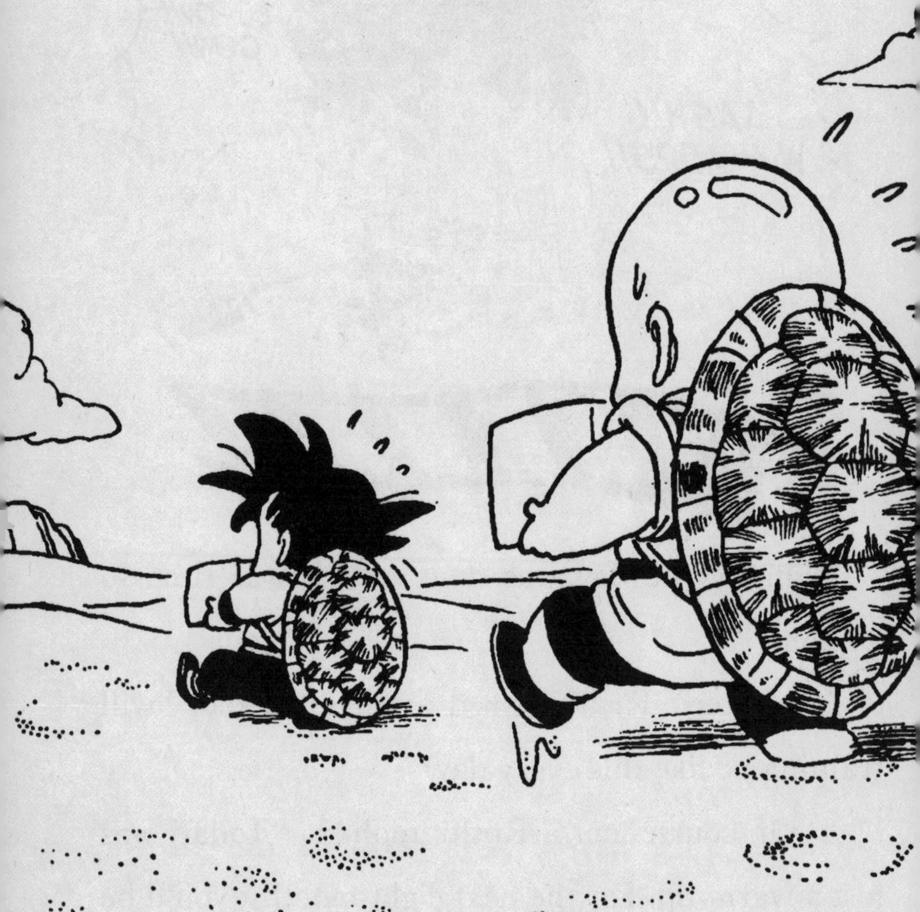

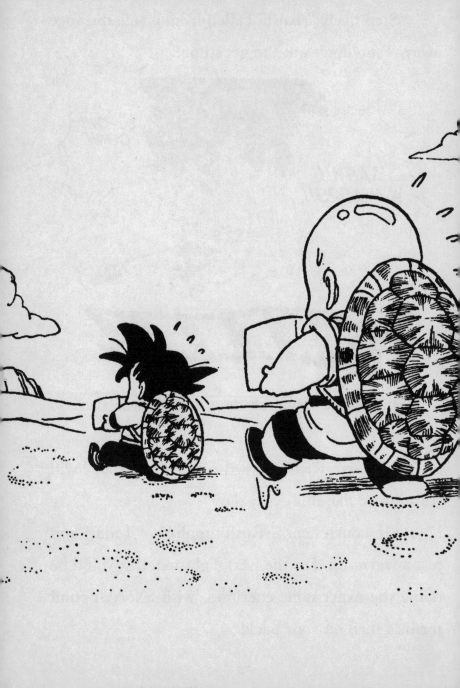

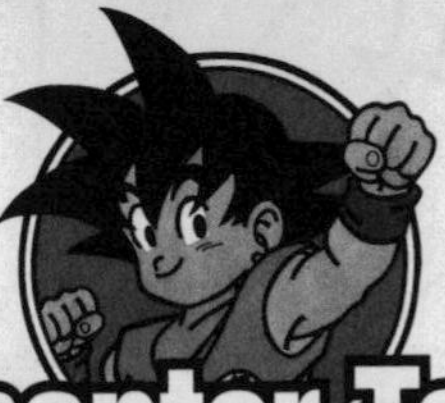

Chapter Ten

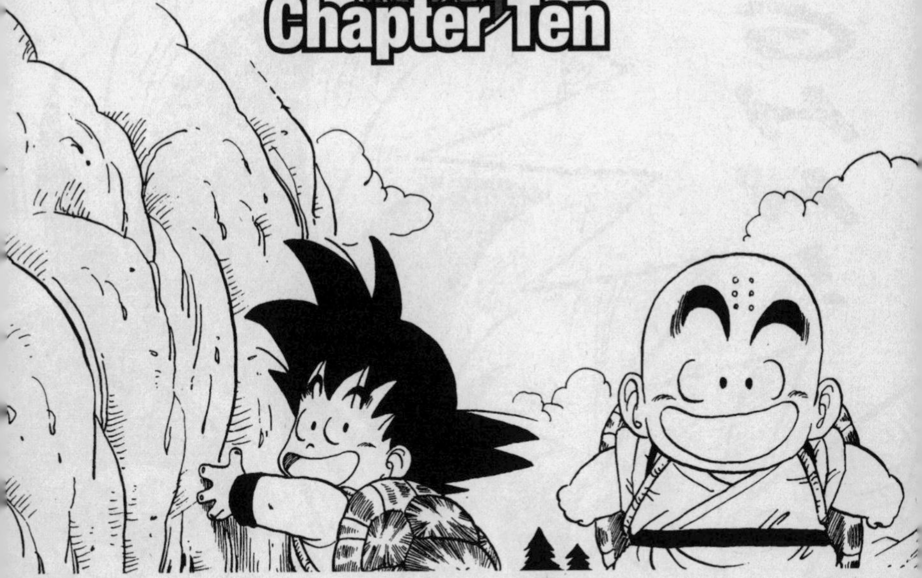

And so it went for the next seven months, exactly as the Turtle Master had promised. The mornings began with the milkrun and ended with the wasps. And through it all, the boys wore the turtle shells on their backs. Little by little, Goku got stronger. Until one day...

"Master, come quick!" Goku cried. "You gotta see this!"

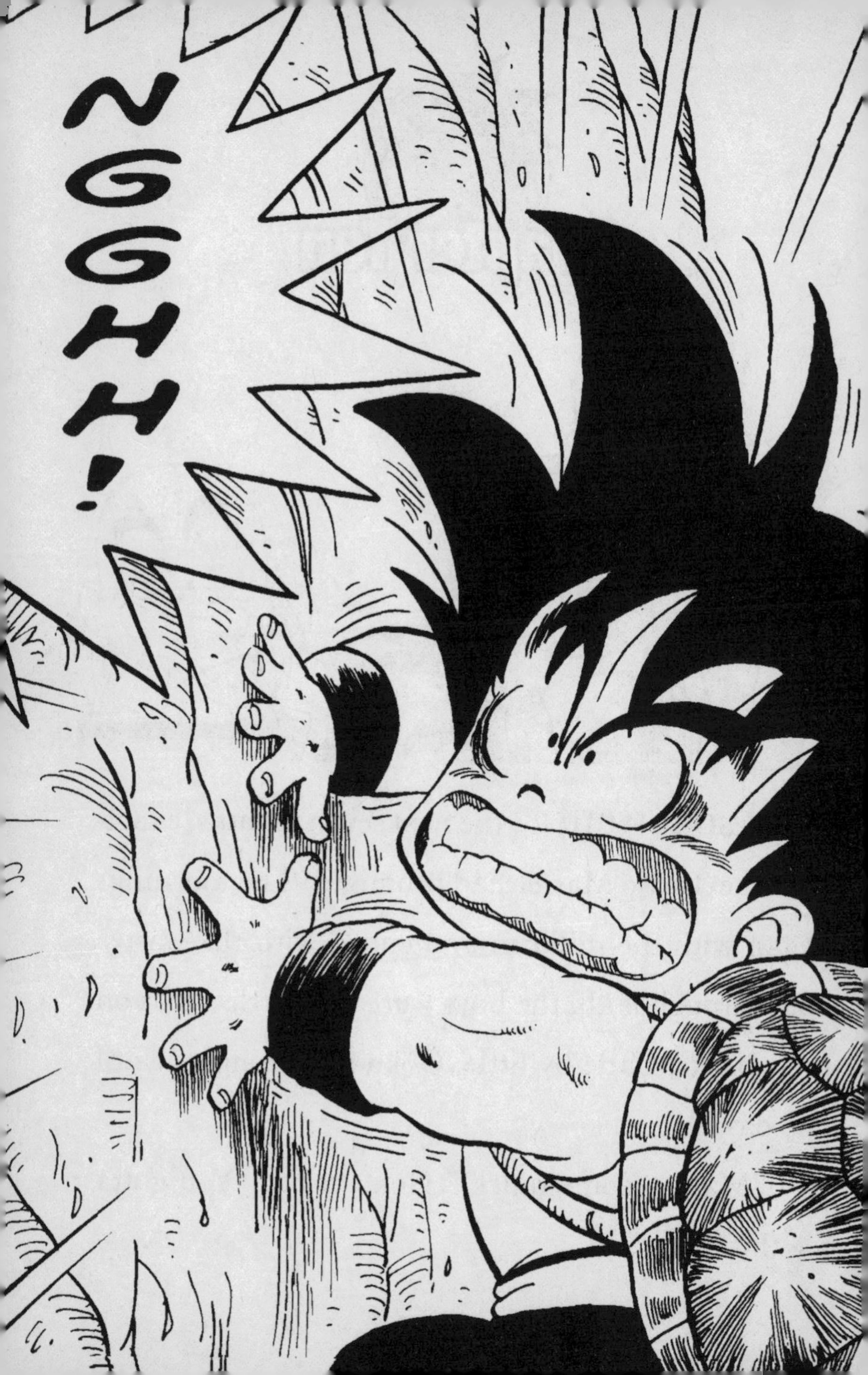
NGGHH!

Goku planted his hands on the humongous stone Master Roshi had challenged them with all those months ago. He leaned into it and pushed with all his might. For a moment, the boulder didn't move. Then slowly–ever so slowly–it shifted. Goku roared and pushed harder. The boulder began to slide.

"Amazing!" the master said.

"My turn, my turn!" Krillin yelled. "I can't move it as far, but..."

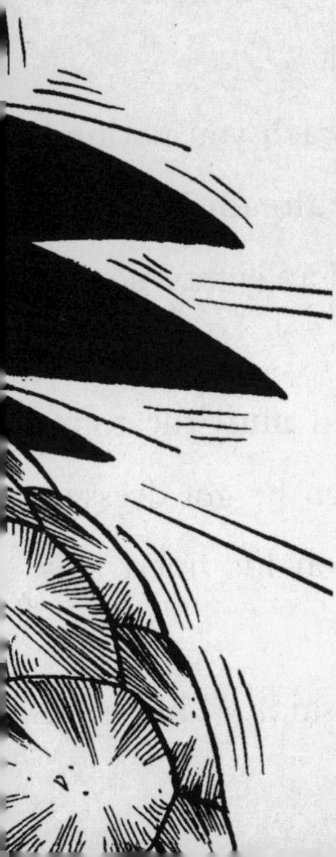

He took Goku's place and pushed with every ounce of strength he had. He pushed until his face turned red and his eyes looked like they were going to pop out of his head.

And the boulder moved! Only a few inches, but it moved!

"Incredible!" the master said.

"Now?" Goku cried. "Now

will you teach us some moves?"

"Well, well," the old master laughed. "I guess it's time to level with you. I never really expected you to move that boulder. I just wanted to keep you motivated. I guess my plan worked better than I thought.

"The truth is," he continued, "there isn't much more I can teach you. Over these past seven months, you've trained until your minds and bodies are as strong and powerful as swords. Now you must learn to focus the power you have gained.

"For this final month, I will teach you nothing new. You will do everything you've already been doing, but this time with the weight of an eighty-pound shell on your back!"

And so the training continued until the tournament was only a day away. When he got dressed that morning, Master Roshi put on his finest suit and hat.

"Well m'lads," the old man said. "This is it.

74

Time to head for the big city. But first, why don't you take off your turtle shells?"

"Whew!" breathed Krillin, unhooking the straps. "What a relief."

"What now, old timer?" Goku asked.

"Why don't you try jumping as high as you can?" Roshi replied.

The boys crouched down, then pushed the ground away. To their amazement, they soared high into the air.

"Goku?" Krillin asked. "Are we really flying?"

When the boys finally landed, they took off running.

"Look at me!" Goku cried,

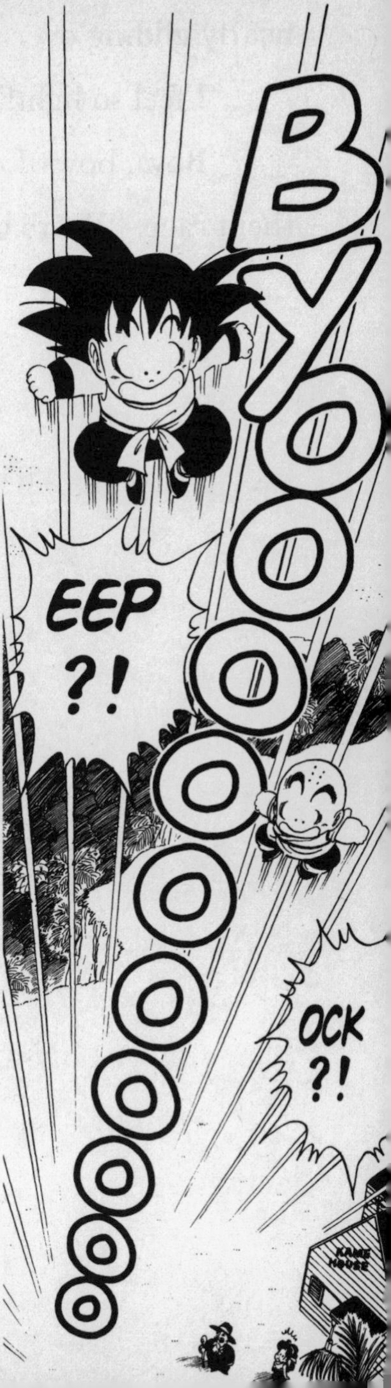
BYOOOOOOOOOOOO
EEP ?!
OCK ?!

nearly gliding over the ground.

"I feel so light!" Krillin echoed.

"Boys, boys! Let's go!" Roshi laughed watching them race. "We're going to miss our flight!"

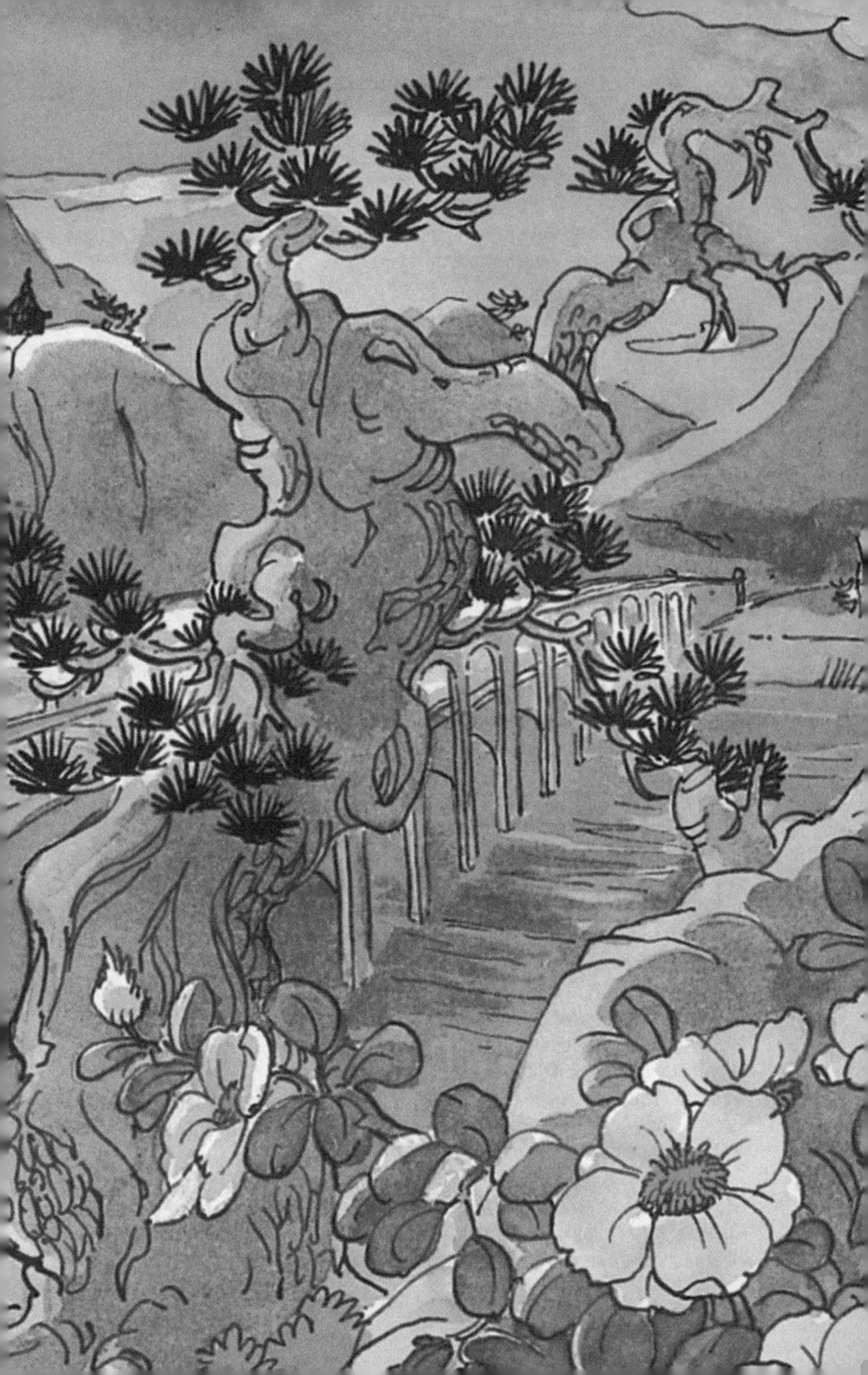

Glossary

Dragon Ball: one of seven mythical orbs that when brought together have the power to summon a wish-granting dragon

Hoi-Poi Capsule: a tiny tube that holds any number of objects—including cars and houses—and releases these objects when thrown on the ground

Kinto'un: a flying cloud that will only carry those who are pure of heart

A Note About Krillin

You may have noticed that Krillin has six small marks on his forehead. When asked about this, Akira Toriyama, the creator of *Dragon Ball*, said that these marks were inspired by the marks he saw on the faces of Chinese monks in movies. This was probably just a bit of movie magic, but some people believe that long ago, a group of monks in China made similar markings on their bodies. The monks are known as the Shaolin.

A monk is a very religious man who lives his life according to the rules of his religion. Shaolin monks practice Buddhism, an ancient religion that began in India. Buddhists try to achieve true knowledge and understanding of all things. One of the ways Buddhists try to do this is by sitting quietly and focusing intently. Legend has it that this practice was brought to the Shaolin by a monk who sat in a cave without moving for nine years! This deep focus is called *meditation*.

Shaolin bring the practice of meditation to their practice of kung fu, a form of self-defense. By concentrating deeply as they fight, the Shaolin are able to withstand incredibly intense pain. Long ago, this made the Shaolin mighty warriors. They protected their temple and defended China against invading armies. Today, the Shaolin monks entertain audiences all over the world with their high-energy kung fu style.

While it's true that Krillin was a monk before he arrived at Master Roshi's island, we don't know for sure whether he's a Shaolin monk. But he definitely has the moves of a martial arts master!

About the Authors

Akira Toriyama
Original Creator of the *Dragon Ball* Manga

Artist/writer Akira Toriyama burst onto the manga (Japanese comics) scene in 1980, with the wildly popular *Dr. Slump*, a science fiction comedy about the adventures of a mad scientist and his android daughter. In 1984 he created the beloved series *Dragon Ball,* which has been translated into many languages, and, as a series, has sold over 150 million copies in Japan. Toriyama-san lives with his family in Japan.

Gerard Jones
Dragon Ball Chapter Book Author

Gerard Jones has been adapting Japanese manga for English-speaking audiences since 1989, including the entire run of *Dragon Ball* comics for VIZ Media and the *Pokémon* comic strip for Creators Syndicate (reprinted by VIZ as *Pikachu Meets the Press*). He has also written hundreds of original comic books for Marvel, DC, and other publishers, and he is the author of several books on popular culture and children's media, including *Killing Monsters* and the Eisner Award-winning *Men of Tomorrow*. He lives in San Francisco with his wife and son, where he works and teaches at the San Francisco Writers Grotto.

Coming Soon...

Book Seven
LET THE TOURNAMENT BEGIN!

After all their training with Master Roshi, Goku and Krillin are ready to rumble. But the fighters in this tournament have moves like none they've ever seen—or smelled. Do the boys have what it takes? Only one way to find out!

vizkids
CHAPTER BOOKS
DRAGON BALL
Let the Tournament Begin!
Based on the original story by Akira Toriyama
Adapted by Gerard Jones
07

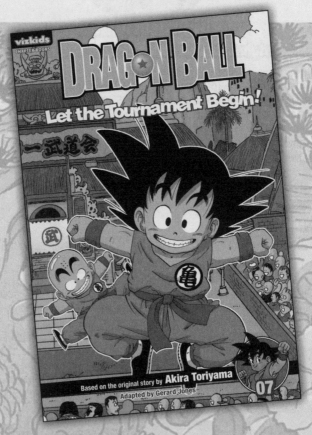